Other books by Mary Mead

The Monarch Beach Mysteries
Out of the Blue (Book 1)
Wild Blue Yonder (Book 2)
Bluebonnets (Book 3)
Deep Blue See (Book 4)

Hot Storage
A Mystery

By Mary Mead

This book is dedicated to Kirk Lee Stenvall
Thanks for the laughs.

Chapter 1

The nose of the Mustang was right up against the barrier that separated the scenic overlook from the Pacific Ocean thirty feet below, providing a 360 degree view of paradise, only the sounds of the surf below and the gulls circling above for company. With the top down it was as good as sitting on the barrier itself only more comfortable.

I unwrapped my Italian sandwich reeking with garlic, onions, peppers, provolone, prosciutto, and salami, all good things not to be eaten in company, and took a huge bite, relishing the chunk of pepper it included.

He came around the barrier, rising up out of the steep slope of scrub brush, and vaulted over the passenger door with ease, sliding right in beside me, leaning close over the console. His right hand slid under my shirt, something cold pressing between my breasts.

"Kiss me," he said, sliding his left hand around my shoulders. "This is a knife. I will use it if I have to." He tapped the blade against my chest.

Stunned beyond belief, I opened my mouth and pushed the chunk of garlic laden sandwich to the forefront between my teeth.

He laughed out loud, surprising both of us. "Chew first, and swallow".

I obeyed but my joy in the sandwich had disappeared along with my saliva. I swallowed several times, trying to choke down the dry bread. He nestled his head into my shoulder and I felt his lips working along my neck, his breath warm against my skin. He was shirtless, his bare chest pressed along my arm, his skin cool against mine. The cold steel blade above my belly was warming, too.

I heard rustling in front of the car, heard scraping and scuffling and heavy breathing, but his head kept me from seeing anything.

"Kiss me," he said again and pressed his mouth against mine. His lips were firm, his breath warm along my cheek.

There was a thump, something banged against the metal barrier and as suddenly as he had appeared, two more men clambered over the railing. One of them lost his balance and lurched against the Mustang, shaking the car. I could hear them even if I couldn't see them.

I was trying to breathe with his mouth pressed to mine.

"Hey!" said the man with the knife, barely lifting his head to glare at the intruders.

"Get a room," replied the bigger of the men, brushing foxtails and bits of weed from his pant legs. "Where did he go?"

My attacker leaned back a little bit, the hand holding the knife pressing a little harder against my breast bone.

"Do I look like a give a shit where your buddy is?"

The big man had the grace to look a little embarrassed, noting the hand under my shirt.

"Sorry, folks," he sighed, "didn't mean to interrupt. This is not the safest place for, um, parking. Did you hear anything, see anyone?"

My guy turned his head slightly, rubbing his nose along my cheek, tenderly kissing my neck.

"I only have eyes for one thing tonight," he said softly, still loud enough for the men to hear.

The second man shouldered around the big guy. "Come on, he had to have taken the long way around. I told you we lost him. Let's get the car."

The bigger man mumbled something I couldn't hear and backed a few steps before he turned and jogged to catch up with his partner who was already half way across the parking area, heading for the road. I could hear their footsteps fade away.

Afraid to move I sat there, trying not to breathe too loud, painfully aware of the man beside me, his left arm still curled around my shoulders, his right fist cradling the handle of the knife that lay heavily against my skin. The silence spread around us and the air began to change color as the sun slid towards the darkening sea.

A minute later he leaned back, shifting into the passenger seat and pulling the knife from under my shirt. I dared to take a deep breath, aware of how tight my throat felt, trying not to cry, willing the muscles in my neck to relax.

"Sorry," he said, turning in the seat to look over my shoulder, back towards the road. "I think they're gone." He brought his eyes back to meet mine. "I had no choice, I really am sorry," he sighed. With a guilty look he pulled a metal comb from under my shirt, turning it back and forth before putting it in his back pocket. He looked around the car.

He lifted my sweat shirt with the zip front from the back seat and pulled it into his lap, turning it so he could slip his arms into the sleeves. I prefer oversize sweatshirts but on him this one was way too tight. The sleeves were ready to split and he couldn't zip the front but he managed to pull it almost closed.

"I'm going to have to borrow this. It's going to get chilly when the sun goes down and I have a long way to go. Don't want my bare skin to show."

Finding my voice for the first time since his abrupt appearance I said, "Take it, it's yours."

Although it was darker now, with the sun setting, I could clearly see dark eyes, almost black in this light, or lack of it, crinkling at the corners as he smiled. The setting sun lit his light colored hair with sparkles of orange.

"I really am sorry," he said again, opening the car door, "I had to scare you to keep you quiet. Those are not very nice men." With one foot already out of the car, he turned and hooked his arm around my neck, pulling me close again. The console bit into my rib cage.

"Have to say, I am not sorry about that kiss. Lady, you know how to kiss" and he kissed me again, just as thoroughly. I responded immediately, leaning into him. If kissing him meant I lived then I could kiss with the best of them. It was a long kiss.

"Take care, babe," he said against my lips, finally pulling his head back.

4

And with that he was gone, back over the side, lost to view in seconds, the sounds of his progress fading until all I could hear was the surf below.

I looked down, where I had squeezed all the spicy fillings for my sandwich into a wet mess in my lap.

~~~

When your work hours are seven to seven it's hard to find time to get away from the job. I found buying a sandwich, a soda and sitting at the view point to watch the sun sink into the sea a relaxing way to end the day.

Not any more. He just ruined it. Unless the top is up and the doors are locked. Maybe a pit bull in the back seat.

Chapter 2

Managing a self-storage facility is never going to be glamorous. All those television shows about the treasures to be found and the fortunes to be made from buying up abandoned storage must be in towns more prosperous than Monarch Beach or Jade Beach. In the time I have been in this business I have seen three units sell for enough to make a profit.

Think about it.

If you had something valuable in storage, and you knew you were going to be short on the rent, wouldn't you, logically, take out the valuables?

If nothing else, sell them for the rent to save the unit. Right?

Most of the units that come up for sale cost more to clean out than the contents can cover. Paying someone to haul the debris to the dump so the unit can be cleaned and rented again is expensive. That's the guy that makes money.

Most of the units that do sell go to dealers, those with a place to sell the assorted pre owned merchandise, usually old clothes. Those with a permanent yard sale or second hand store may eventually turn over their investment.

Me? Not worth my time.

The attraction to managing a facility with on site management is the free rent, which is not free. Rent is charged monthly, then credited on your paycheck. You never see the money so your rent is never late. Utilities are free.

The pay is usually much less than minimum wage if you work it out hourly.

Couples are preferred because if each one works forty hours a week, eighty hours are covered without having to pay overtime by staggering the hours. It's a hard job to get and an even harder one to leave. You never save enough money to pay first, last and deposits on a new place.

Read stuck.

In my case, I was lucky.

My former husband split for a more glamorous life, one that did not include a wife or a storage facility. Ironic, since he was the one who wanted the job.

I had turned an unprofitable mess into a profitable business in the year we had been there and the owners wanted to keep me. I also had my veteran's benefits from my twenty years in the Army so I was comfortable with the situation.

When Sporticus, my ex, left, the owners agreed to keep me as a single. They also approved a part timer for weekends, giving me those off. By hiring a guy for weekends, I could assign him any heavy work I couldn't do. My reward for a job well done.

The owners were a partnership - a father and his two grown sons. The Murphy's, father and sons, were great employers. We had an excellent working relationship - I took care of their business and they stayed out of mine. As long as the facility continued to make a profit they left me alone.

Besides Beach Storage, the family owned a tool rental business, the latter including everything from card tables to moving vans, lawn mowers to tents. In addition they owned a local landmark, the Gem of the Ocean, which sounds exotic while in actuality it's a beer and pizza place, the local watering hole in the neighboring Monarch Beach. Locals like to tell you they're going to the Gem because it sounds like gym, giving you the impression they are going to work out when actually the only lifting they intend to do involves slices of pizza and beer mugs.

The older son, Paul, my immediate supervisor, the one I called if I needed something, managed the tool rental business. He could be found Tuesday through Saturday behind the counter or lazing in the sun just outside. You know him or at least one like him.

He's the guy that hits forty and suddenly sprouts a ponytail and gold chains. The top two buttons on his shirts never close. Half the time a sporty new car takes up residence in his driveway, always the life of the party.

I've heard Paul is known to party pretty hard south of us, keeping his escapades away from town.

As long as my paychecks were on time and didn't bounce, I could care less.

I preferred the patriarch of the clan, Shamus. He was a dead ringer for Santa Claus in both attitude and appearance. Short and stout, crowned with a billowing mop of snow white hair and a sparkling white beard he was everyone's idea of the perfect Grandpa.

He managed the Gem although he could be found most mornings at Kelly's Diner in Monarch, breakfasting with his cronies, old timers and retirees that gathered there every morning, no matter the weather, to solve the world's problems.

The locals called him Papa Smurf. He spent as much time at the diner as he did in the office, leaving most of the business in the hands of the bartenders and barmaids. The younger son, Patrick, I had yet to meet.

Patrick, known locally as Trick, for his ability to avoid any attachment to the female population. According to the locals he had dated and dumped every female within the town limits between the ages of 20 and 50.

His dating record reached legendary status among the old timers, who counted him up there with Brad Pitt when it came to the ladies.

My dealings with men being of the negative variety, I didn't give a fig if I ever met him.

One thing did concern me. The family occupied half a dozen units at my facility, using them to store inventory for the other businesses. One was designated for family belongings, such as Christmas decorations, seasonal displays, that type of thing.

Colleen, the matriarch, had two units for herself to accommodate her personal collection of whatever. She was always on the lookout for an empty unit she could confiscate and use to extend her storage space.

I was under threat of death from all three male Murphy's to keep her from adding another unit. It led to a running game of hide the empties. If she found one she promptly moved in, grabbing something, anything from her car or unit and taking possession.

The perpetual game of hide and seek added a little spice to the day.

Soft job, yes, one that requires a certain type of person – combination accountant, salesman, landscaper and all around handy man. Someone who is comfortable alone, at ease with long periods of solitude and at the same time sociable with all age groups.

Still, it was long hours. Although I might have no customers all day, I still had to be present in case someone needed help.

Surprising how many people lost their keys and could not access their belongings, expecting me to have an extra key since we provided a free lock with each rental.

Many wanted me to keep an extra key on file in the office so they didn't have to keep track of their keys.

No way. Sure lawsuit there by claiming I used their key to garner their assets and sell them.

The people you meet in this job are a true cross section of America, more so than any other business. From the homeless, looking for a place to keep their cans and the things their shopping carts won't hold, to the millionaires remodeling their palaces up on the hill. One good thing about people – they will not get rid of their stuff unless forced. Even then it's a crap shoot.

One of my customers, an elderly gentleman, rented a small space to keep his books – four boxes of them. I know because I helped him unload them, afraid his arm would snap off just getting them out of the trunk of his car.

His rent was paid promptly every month and he came in regularly, once a week, to pick up two or three books and replace the two or three from last week, sort of a small private lending library.

I asked him once why he didn't just take them home. The answer? His wife didn't want them collecting dust at home. I suggested the library. His response? He had one. In his unit.

A gentleman of the old school, he always dressed in a suit, complete with pocket hankie and a tie, when he came to visit his books. I had no idea of his age although I kept an eye on him when he was inside the gates, concerned a gust of wind off the beach might catch him like a kite and send him sailing still clutching a book.

Another was a famous writer, who rented a space for his original manuscripts and first editions in case of fire or burglary at his home. I suspected I was one of two facilities keeping his them safe.

All kinds.

Renters were required to have a current driver's license, which we copied and kept on file and a physical street address. We also reserved the right to refuse service to anyone.

Posting a prominent sign in the office announcing our full cooperation with local law enforcement helped eliminate some of the less desirable, especially with the warning that we would open any unit on request without benefit of a search warrant. Access to management was spelled out in the individual contracts, in bold print, specifically noting in several places that management could, and might, enter any unit without previous notice.

Another sign notified anyone who could read that drug sniffing dogs practiced on the premises. Even with all these precautions there were drug dealers positive they could beat the odds and keep their product in the units. I had on two occasions found the door to a unit lined inside with cockroach traps in the mistaken belief that drug sniffing dogs would not smell drugs over the traps.

In my years of management I have also busted up a prostitution ring using one of my units as a miniature brothel, a shady lawyer hiding his files, and a credit card duplicating scam.

The worst are the Sunday morning couples.

They meet at the bar on Friday night, spend the night drinking, Saturday is given to whooping it up and by Sunday they are forever in love and moving in together, usually in a local motel. They can't keep their hands off each other, pay no attention to the rules I explain and rent a unit to combine their belongings until the wedding.

I will only put one name on the account for a specific reason. Only one of them has control. That person can give the other one permission to access the unit. They can also cancel said access at any given time. They usually miss that part, too.

They spend Sunday moving stuff into the unit and squashing themselves together every chance they get plus giggling. There's always giggling. And drinking. Either it's a hair of the dog, or a pick me up, they're at it all day.

They begin to sober up by Monday night, fight by Tuesday, and by Wednesday whoever has their name on the account is barring the other one from access.

Thursday the one locked out will show up wanting to get their stuff, and the dance begins anew, explaining the rules they ignored on Sunday to suck face.

Friday they reach an agreement and come in to remove their crap, barely speaking. They forfeit their twenty dollar deposit for failure to give notice, fight over whose fault it is and argue with me for at least twenty minutes over why they should get a refund.

They finally leave, I clean the unit and on Saturday we start all over again.

I have one woman who came in three consecutive Sundays, each time with a different guy and pulled this same stunt. I refused to rent to her on the fourth Sunday and she went somewhere else, leaving a stream of foul language following along like the contrail of a passing jet.

I made money on the deal with multiple rents on the same unit plus forfeiture of the deposit. It just gets old listening to the whining. I was happy to leave most of it to Steve, the weekend guy. A very nice older man who loved to talk. To anyone. Or anything. I was pretty sure he talked to the plants when left alone.

You just never knew who was going to come through the door next.

T. Tom Tanner, the lead singer for the country band T Three is a customer and an absolute joy. He is friendly, polite, and eye candy to boot. So is his wife, Tee, lest you get the wrong idea. They are really down to earth nice people, always taking time to ask after my health and taking the time to listen to the response.

Adding to the mix are the regulars, the customers you see frequently. A little kindness and a little foresight can improve your security by using their observations.

Randy is an excellent example.

He worked out of his unit for years before I took over, a blatant abuse of the rules. Storage units are for storage only – not for small businesses, manufacturing or quilting groups. No band practice.

City regulations specifically deny working in a unit. Insurance companies also frown on the practice, citing the various dangers to the premises.

There are so many tricks in this trade the more you know the better manager you are. Believe me, the best asset for a successful storage facility is an honest manager who knows the ropes.

In Randy's case, he had gotten away with doing what he wanted for so long, he thought he could tell me what to do.

I asked him politely, the first time, to cease working in his unit, which he referred to as "the shop."

The second time I cautioned him he didn't even bother to respond, just turned a meaty shoulder and went right past me.

The third time, when his gate code was locked, he tailgated behind another truck to sneak in unseen.

First, I saw him on the camera.

Second, tailgating is verboten for strike two.

Third, when he snuck around behind the building to avoid the cameras and access his unit, he found two bright yellow overlocks blocking any attempt to reach his own lock and open the door.

When yelling at me didn't help, he stormed off.

The next day he tried wheedling, and then stomped off. The third day he tried bribery, bringing me a hamburger and a sweet tea.

By the fourth day he was waving the white flag, desperate to get to his stuff.

Randy's unit was against the fence, in the far back corner of the lot, a long way from the front gate and the office. He had no family, no job, other than the work he did in his unit, and nowhere else to go. Without access to his unit he was completely lost.

So I made a deal with him. He could work in his unit as long as no one else knew it. If another customer was back in that section, he had to shut it down until the coast was clear.

In return, if he saw anyone acting in a suspicious manner, he called the office and told me.

It worked out well for both of us. He was instrumental in breaking up the prostitution ring and a couple attempting to live in their unit by giving me a heads up.

He regained a place to go every day. I had a spy in the back lot.

Another great customer was Marty, who helped with any electrical problems in return for earlier access to get his crew to the job sites on time.

It's pretty much the old barter system in action.

And don't get me wrong. The majority of my customers are like a holiday – some turkeys, some hams and some festive nuts.

There are also a few rotten apples – those that think a woman alone is fair game and they are the mighty hunter.

Those, too, come in all guises.

Milt, a longtime customer, he and his wife both in their seventies or so, always polite and friendly, always paid on time, great customers for years. Eventually he gave notice he was vacating the unit. On his final day he came to the office to tell me he had spread a blanket down in the back of his van so I could come up and get a personal thank you.

You just never know.

~~~

Another detriment to abusing the property is a random walk through. I check every night in a random pattern. Sometimes I walk, sometimes I use the company golf cart, sometimes just a drive through in my car. I check the doors, to be sure they are locked and secure.

The golf cart is electric, makes very little noise. It also carries a large trash can and a broom so I can pick up the odd bits of trash and cigarette butts that customers toss on the grounds or behind buildings.

I check at different times, early or late, and never in a set pattern.

I also enjoy the quiet, once the lot is empty. It's nice to toodle around in the little electric cart, making my own breeze in my face, while checking that all is well in my little world.

I have thought about getting a dog, for companionship as well as extra security but so far not willing to make that commitment.

After the incident last week I avoided my favorite after hours view from the overlook and settled for my evening trips around the lot. The middle of the month is pretty quiet since rents are all due on the first.

At the time only three units were available for rent and they were popular sizes that should rent quickly.

As a rule, I keep empty units tagged with little wire tags on the door. The bright yellow tags are easy to spot and quickly snap off when I need to show the unit.

Mrs. Murphy hasn't figured that out.

Yet.

Chapter 3

Monday nights my rounds are a little hurried from September to January.

I am a huge fan of the NFL. Monday night football is my 'date night' – I have a standing date with a pizza and the game.

This particular Monday night was no different. I had ordered the pizza, the beer was cold, and I wanted to get inside, kick off my shoes, and watch football.

On my last lap, the far aisle, something caught my eye and I backed up and turned down the row.

What looked like a plastic bag quivered beside a unit door. Enough to catch my attention.

It wasn't moving, just shivering and shaking in the slight breeze from the nearby ocean. I drove that way, intent on grabbing it from the cart and continuing to my pizza.

I leaned down to snag it and stopped.

It wasn't a bag.

It was a long strip of packing tape, the reinforced kind with the threads running through it.

It had snagged under the door, stuck on something inside the unit and now the loose end flapped around.

I had to get off the cart and tug to try to release it.

No go.

Checking the unit number so I could make a note on the account, I realized there was no lock on the door.

Clients do move without giving notice, contrary to the rental agreement they signed. They forfeit their deposit when they do. I slipped the latch back and stepped inside to see if they had also left trash or debris inside, another common occurrence when customers move out.

It was hard to see in the dark so I waited till my eyes adjusted. The unit was clean.

Until I turned around to leave.

Nestled up close to the front wall, beside the door, was a stack of cartons, three stacks of three. Each of them was wrapped in clear, heavy plastic, the plastic strapped with strips of reinforced packing tape, the kind with the strings embedded.

The bottom carton nearest the door had a strip of the tape torn loose. When the tape tore it carried a long strip of plastic with it. One end was connected under the carton, the other ran under the door and into my hand. I tugged on my end of the tape and nothing happened. The carton didn't even shift.

I reached up and shook the top carton, to see if anything was in it. It had enough weight that I could tell it wasn't empty.

With a sigh I carefully lifted it down, not wanting the heavy carton to fall on my head. When I got it on the floor I used the edge of a key to tear a hole in the plastic sheeting. Wiggling a finger under the plastic I managed to tear it along the edge of a tape strip until I had enough loose to pull it clear. The tape refused to give, clinging to the plastic. I had to peel the plastic between strips of tape, unwinding it all the way around by turning the carton. It took some time to work the plastic sleeves off the ends of the carton.

I was finally able to get to the center seam and split it with the key. Inside were tightly wrapped smaller packs, a little larger than a standard red brick, packed closely together. I counted twelve bricks in the top layer.

I pulled one out and stepped back to the door, unable to see what the wrapping concealed. Just outside the door there was enough illumination from our security lights to see what I held.

Either someone planned an enormous bake off or flour was on the endangered species list. I doubted both. Pretty sure I had nine cases of cocaine or some similar drug. Great.

I put the package on top of the nearest carton and locked up the unit, using one of the heavy Master locks from the cart. Once the door was secure, I turned on the cart and headed for the office. I stuck the original strip of tape and plastic into my back pocket and went to call the police. So much for football and pizza.

The first officers to respond were shown the unit and promptly called for detectives.

I made a pot of coffee and settled in the office. While I waited for the detectives I pulled the strip of plastic out of my pocket and looked at it again in the brighter lights of the office.

The tape strip stuck to the plastic was impossible to tear cross wise, easy to tear length wise, between the embedded strings. I've seen a lot of it. Whatever this brand was, the three center strings in the tape were colored. Red, white and green, giving it a holiday flair.

Tugging on it I was sure you could hold a Christmas tree to the wall with this stuff.

The detectives finally arrived, followed by a van and over the next hours photographed, labeled and removed the cartons.

For my part I answered the same questions three times.

Seriously.

I was to the point I questioned the wisdom of calling it in. Maybe I could have just lugged the cartons to the street and claimed ignorance.

I printed out copies of gate access during the last twenty four hours and burned a couple of DVDs from our computerized camera system and handed them over, keeping copies for my own records.

The unit containing the contraband (their word, not mine) according to my records was empty.

Some person or persons unknown had snapped off the little yellow tag and stacked up the cartons. The door to the unit had been blocked from the camera's view by a white van and a U-Haul rental truck during the daylight hours, no way to tell which if either had unloaded into the unit.

Also on a corner, it could have been accessed by anyone in the lot, not necessarily the van or truck.

Plus, I had not checked that unit last night, so it was quite possible that the cartons had been unloaded the day before.

And so it went.

It was well after midnight when the detectives came in to tell me they were through for the night, and would see me bright and early the next morning. Oh, goody.

They had their own lock for the door, so I gave them a temporary code to access the gate, shut down the computers and locked up.

It was one o'clock in the morning. I decided to grab whatever sleep I could and do my reports Tuesday morning.

~~~

The unlocked door and the abandoned cartons of drugs kept me from sleeping so I was up, dressed, and in the office early. I wrote up reports of last night's events, added copies of all the information I had given the police and made a file.

I sent one copy of the whole file to the owner, printed out a hard copy for the office, and saved the whole thing to an online service I use for backup.

Checking the log, the police had been in and out several times since the gates opened. I pulled up the camera closest to the unit and sure enough, one police cruiser and one unmarked Ford sedan were parked in the aisle.

I made coffee and watched them move around while it dripped.

Our camera system has twelve cameras strategically located around the grounds, all in living color although we don't have sound. It's still pretty easy to figure out what's going on without hearing them.

For instance, the guy sneaking around the corner of the building, looking in all directions first, and coming back out with a wet spot on his zipper is definitely not using the restroom we provide for the customer's convenience.

He will also be getting a request to wash down the building, which he will ignore, and a ten dollar fine, which he will pay or move his stuff out.

Usually the embarrassment of being caught does the job.

Sipping coffee and watching the police was at least something new and different. Even that paled after a while and I returned to my trusty Kindle.

A little before noon two men in suits pulled up inFord and came into the office. They showed their gold badges and ID and we all shook hands.

I offered coffee and they accepted. We all sat down to become best friends.

Once the prenuptials were out of the way, the biggest guy took the lead. He was heavy set but not fat, balding, and looked like your average citizen, except for the gun under his arm. And the suit, a deep navy blue, highlighted by a white shirt and a purple tie. Jeans and sweatshirts or tee shirts were the most common uniform in Jade Beach.

He introduced himself as Karl Miller and his credentials backed him up. He was with the DEA.

His partner was smaller, more compact, with a similar suit and credentials. I didn't have time to read his name before he pulled them back and tucked them in an inside pocket. I thought about pulling out my driver's license and flashing it and decided they might not appreciate it.

When everyone was settled Agent Miller pulled out a small notebook and flipped pages.

"I've been over everything we found last night. Do you have anything you can add to the report? Any way to identify who moved the drugs in?"

"No, sir," I said, shaking my head. "I gave you a copy of my own report for my owners. That's everything I have." Reaching into a drawer, I pulled out one of the yellow tags I use for empty units. "This is the kind of tag I put on the hasps of the empty units," I explained, handing it to him. "As you can see, once it's clipped on, it's just a simple snap to remove it. The wire hanger is crimped, easy to snap off."

He nodded and made a noise in his throat. His partner stood up and went over to the wall to admire the picture of Troy Aikman in full gear that adorned that wall. "You go to this game?" he asked.

"No, sir. The photographer is a friend. He made me a copy because I was a huge Aikman fan."

"Cowboys fan?"

"Since 1960. Not fond of the current regime but always a fan."

Detective Miller cleared his throat and I pulled my attention back to him.

"Well, here's the deal," he began, folding up his notebook. "We've been working with a state wide drug enforcement task force. It includes several different law enforcement agencies, including your local police. They have their own representative who will be contacting you. We are asking that you keep this to yourself as much as possible. We want this stopped."

I nodded and motioned him to continue.

"Those cartons, the ones you found last night, match the shipment we managed to catch in Oceanside six months ago. I'll skip the details, for now. We're hoping these guys may want these back so we're not going to draw any more attention to this incident. The cartons have been replaced in that unit, as close as possible to their original placement. There will be no reports in the paper or on television. If possible we'd like to leave that unit as it is, for a while, see what happens."

"That's fine," I said. "I can put it in our system as under repair, so no one else is going to bother it. Is there anything else I can do?"

"There is another thing. What we would like to do is put a guy inside. Here, at your facility."

"What is this guy going to do? Sit in the office and try to look like a fichus?"

Agent Miller smiled and folded his hands. "The man we're sending has been working this case for almost a year, undercover. We don't want him identified, so we're hoping you can add him as an employee. A groundskeeper, assistant, whatever. Something that will allow him full access to the property at all hours without being an obvious plant. Someone that your customers won't question."

"Do I have to pay him?" I asked, thinking the owners are going to balk.

Again with the smile. "No, ma'am. You just need to provide a cover story for him if your other customers ask. We want him to have twenty-four hour access if there's a way to do that. He'll just be around."

So here's the thing.

This nice DEA agent is explaining his plan, to put an able bodied man on the premises whose presence can be justified.

That's what he's saying.

What I am hearing is they want to bring a guy in here to do all the sweeping, which I hate, climb the ladders to change light bulbs, oil doors, and all the other maintenance around the facility.

For free.

"I can put him in as a maintenance man, as long as he doesn't mind a lot of sweeping," I said, trying to keep a straight face. "We can work out an access code to allow him to come in at night although that will be noticeable. Our gates normally lock at seven. I'll have to get creative to explain him after hours. He'll have to be unobtrusive."

The other detective guffawed from across the room.

Agent Miller gave him a look and turned back to me.

"That would be fine, ma'am. He'll get together with you and set his own hours. He won't interfere I assure you. We really appreciate your cooperation."

"When will he start?"

Agent Miller stood up and pushed in his chair, glancing at the other guy, who was already headed for the door.

"That will be up to him, ma'am. I can't give you an exact time. I don't know his schedule. He will be in touch with you."

"He's gonna have to if he wants an access code."

"Again, you can make all the arrangements with him. And thank you again. We appreciate your cooperation. Here's my card," he said, extending it to me. "If you think of anything else please give me a call. If you have any other problems, please don't hesitate to call. Again, the local police will also contact you."

Standing up, I offered my hand. "Thank you, sir. Believe me, I appreciate your efforts. The last thing I want is drugs here. I worked too hard to clean this place up."

I followed them to the door and watched them get into their car and leave.

I managed not to dance a jig.

Until they were out of sight.

I wrote up a quick email for the owner, explaining the new guy on the premises and fired it off. Once the gates locked up for the night I headed for the grocery store.

I needed more coffee.

Chapter 4

Home was an apartment above the office.

The original building had the office upstairs, above the units, with a staircase climbing up the outside. At some point, an addition to the building enclosed the staircase, creating a tunnel between the two halves. Upstairs became the new living quarters while the office was relocated at the bottom of the stairs.

Makes for an easy commute to work.

The enclosed stairs are nice when it's raining.

Not so good when you forget to the turn on the porch light and it's dark. Then you're faced with an ominous black cavern that depends on reflected light from the parking lot.

With all the drug business I forgot to turn on the porch light at the top of the stairs.

Carrying two bags of groceries I started up that long, dark void.

I was half way up when I realized there was something at the top. Something hunkered against my front door. I have seen cats, dogs, possums and a raccoon mistake my stairs for a nice place to live. Twice bats have dive bombed me.

Whatever or whoever was up there was large enough to cover the bottom third of the door. Not a bat. Using the trick of looking to the side of the object I couldn't identify it, just a darker shade of dark.

It wasn't moving.

I backed up carefully and made it to the bottom stair.

Setting the grocery bags on the bench at the foot of the stairs I tried to make out what was against the door.

I hoped it wasn't a bear.

I pulled my keys from my pocket. There is a mini mag light on my key chain, one of those little ones that come free in advertisements. I shined it up the stairs at the door. It was a feeble light but better than nothing.

Something black hung from my doorknob.

Something with a zipper.

Easing up the stairs I reached out and touched it. Lifted it off the doorknob and carried it back down to the light.

My sweatshirt.

Last seen around the torso of the guy at the beach.

Somehow, he had found me.

I went back up and unlocked the door, turned on the porch light and retrieved my groceries. Back inside, I locked the door behind me.

With the lights on I felt better.

I put the groceries away and started some water for tea. While that was heating I picked up the sweatshirt.

It smelled fresh and clean, that distinct, unique scent of laundry dried outdoors. This guy either lived with his mom or in a campground. Checking the pockets I found nothing.

Just a freshly laundered sweatshirt returned.

With the lights on I opened the front door and checked the stairs again. Still nothing. I double locked the door.

I still didn't sleep well that night.

Bright sunshine the next morning put things in a better perspective.

I had my sweatshirt back. While not a fortress my apartment was secure. More so than many places because of the facility's gates and camera system. The security software was also loaded on my home computer so I could check the grounds from home without having to go back to the office.

How he found me I had no clue. The only possibility I could think of was something left in the pocket of the sweatshirt, something with my address on it.

When I opened the office I backed up the video cameras and checked last night's footage. There is no camera on the stairs or that corner of the building. The other cameras yielded nothing out of the ordinary.

My late night visitor had managed to avoid all the cameras.

~~~

Everyone who works with the public understands what a pain in the fanny it is to have someone come in five minutes before closing. One more reason I don't own a gun.

I had already closed out the computer for the day when a beach god wandered in. Being a beach community we're used to the slim hipped, heavy shouldered great looking guys with the sun tipped hair and the warm golden tan no spray booth ever gets right.

This one had thick rust colored hair with gold highlights, just a little long, touching the collar of his sweatshirt. He flipped his sunglasses up to rest on top of his head.

Launching my standard 'sorry, we're closed, come back tomorrow speech' I was cut off mid-sentence when he lifted the bottom of his sweatshirt and displayed the gold badge clipped to his waistband.

"I assume you're not here to rent a unit," I said.

"No, ma'am. I'm John Kincaid, with Monarch PD. I'm the local liaison officer with the county drug force. I believe Detective Miller told you I would be contacting you. Just wanted to drop by, introduce myself and see if you have anything to add to the report you filled out."

"No, sir, sorry. That was everything I had."

"And very thorough, I might add. Believe me, we appreciate it."

He had dark eyes, like chocolate, warm and melting.

"You're welcome," I said.

He folded his arms and leaned on top of the counter. "I understand DEA is going to put a guy in here. Undercover."

I thought we were supposed to keep that under wraps but what the heck, not my job. "Yes, sir. That's what they told me."

"He's not in place yet?"

"No, sir, he hasn't checked in with me."

Kincaid reached over and ran a forefinger through the bowl of peppermints on the counter.

"My father is sir," he smiled. "You can call me John."

"Fine, John," I said. "I still haven't seen the other guy."

The detective straightened up, giving the counter a pat with both hands. "All right, then. I'll check back with you in a few days. If anything should come up, give me a call." He reached into a back pocket and pulled out a card that he slid across to me. "My cell number is on the back, if I'm not at the station. Call any time."

He somehow managed to make that sound like an invitation.

"Will do," I said, moving around the counter to escort him out and lock up behind him.

He took the hint and went to the door, which I held open for him.

"You take care now, Mrs. ?"

"Miss," I corrected, and stuck out my hand. "Montoya. Marlena Montoya."

He shook my hand, his own firm and a little callused. "Miss Montoya, then."

"Marlena is fine," I said.

"Okay, Marlena, nice to meet you. I'll check in with you from time to time. I don't think we'll see them again. Once they've been spotted they'll shift the trail. If you have any questions or if I can be of any assistance, just call."

"Sure thing," I said, and opened the door a little wider.

With a nod, he finally stepped outside. I closed and locked the door, turned off the lights and closed the blinds, to finish the evening routine. I picked up my keys and the deposit bag.

There was something familiar about Detective Kincaid, something I couldn't quite place. Not unusual in a small town. I had probably seen him at Kelly's, the local diner or the grocery store over the ridge in

Monarch Beach. It would come to me, or in all probability, I would run into him again.

Jade Beach and Monarch Beach are both small towns separated by a ridge that runs from the hills into the ocean, breaking into steep cliffs where it meets the water. Jade is home port for a small fishing fleet as well as larger boats that put in for supplies and repairs. The twin docks there are always busy. Monarch is smaller and has no industry. However, it does have town amenities, such as a post office, police station, hardware store and two grocery stores among others. It was a safe bet we'd meet again.

On the way to the bank I wondered if I should have mentioned the sweatshirt left on my door, then decided it had no bearing on the case. My adventure with the guy on the beach had nothing to do with cases of drugs in my storage units. I had never reported the beach incident.

With a shrug I forgot about it and made the deposit.

~~~

Saturday was pretty busy, customers in and out all day. Being a weekend Steve, the weekend manager, was on duty in the office leaving me free to get to some weeding, a chore I was eager to pass on to the undercover guy.

I knocked off and went upstairs before the office closed. Steve was a talker. If he caught me I would be hung up in conversation for another hour. I went upstairs and ordered a pizza. I deserved it having put in a good day in the flowerbeds. Besides the last one I didn't get to enjoy.

I jumped into the shower while I waited for the delivery.

I pulled on sweats after I dried off, checked the television guide for movies and found an old Thin Man classic starring William Powell and Myrna Loy. I love the old movies, films that depended on good writing and better acting instead of special effects.

I grabbed a beer and some napkins, made myself a nice little set up on the coffee table and settled in to wait for dinner.

When I heard someone on the stairs, I used the pause feature to stop the movie so I could pay the delivery guy. The money was already laid out on the table.

Opening the door, I froze.

Money in hand, hand extended to pay, I stood there with my mouth open.

The delivery guy was familiar.

Very familiar.

From the blond hair to the dark eyes.

The borrower of the sweatshirt stood on the third step down, balancing a pizza box in one hand. In the other he was holding up a folding wallet with an ID card and a gold badge.

"Before you scream, or kick me down the stairs," he said, "I can explain." Even the voice was familiar, warm and seductive.

"You have one minute." I kept my hand on the door in case I needed to slam it.

"Whoa, gonna take longer than that, ma'am. Here, can you take this?"

"Is this your official job?" I asked, taking the pizza from him. I had to let go of the door to do so. It was a large pizza. "Or did you just threaten him with your comb?"

"No, ma'am, we got here at the same time. I volunteered to bring it up."

"I hope you paid him," I said, turning to set the box on the table.

"Yes, I did," he said, stepping up to the open door. "I even tipped him."

I took a couple of steps back.

He moved on into the entry, shutting the door behind him.

I grabbed my phone and stepped back closer to the table, keeping some distance between us.

"My ID," he said, handing over the wallet.

According to the information in my hand, this was Detective Declan Burke of the California Criminal Investigation Division. If it wasn't real it was the best counterfeit I ever saw. Even the picture was good.

I handed it back to him.

"May I come in?"

"You appear to be in, Mr. Burke."

"Please, call me Declan," he said. "After all, we do know each other."

"Do you want to explain? My dinner is getting cold."

I waited, folding my arms.

"Okay. I can do that. It's going to take a few minutes. How about sharing your dinner?"

"You sure are pushy," I said.

What the heck, he was a cop. "Come on in, grab a plate. The napkins are on the coffee table. Do you want a beer? Soda?"

"What are you having?" He stepped over and slid two slices on to a plate, then moved into the living room and set it on the coffee table.

I went into the kitchen, tucked a beer under my arm, picked up another plate and joined him.

He had pulled off his jacket and rolled up his sleeves. "This is great," he said, looking at the television screen. "Are you watching this?"

"I was," I said.

"The Thin Man? I love these movies! Which one is this?"

Terrific. I pushed the pause button and froze the screen.

"Hate to disappoint you," I said. "Explanation?"

He seriously looked disappointed. With a sigh, he sat down. "Can we eat first?"

"I can," I said, picking up a slice and grabbing a napkin.

"You're not gonna give me a break, are you?"

"Not on purpose," I said.

He actually grinned at me. "Okay, tough girl. I'm part of a state wide drug enforcement task force. I've been undercover for over a year." He paused to take a swallow of beer. "Those guys at the beach were bad guys. I was running from them, obviously. If they had caught me it would have blown the whole operation. I had to get clear. You were there. You know the rest."

I chewed pizza and thought for a minute. Seemed possible.

"Is that an apology?"

He chuckled and reached for his beer. "No, this is," he said, pointing at his plate. "I am sorry. I thought I said that before. Sorry I scared you." With a twinkle in his dark eyes he added, "I'm still not sorry about that kiss."

I felt the blush creeping up my neck.

"Apology accepted," I said. "Eat your pizza."

He leaned to pick up his plate and grab a napkin. "Do I get the movie, too?"

"Anyone ever tell you no?"

"Often," he chuckled. "Come on, toughie. I'm hungry and I love this movie, one of my all-time favorites. We don't have to talk."

He won. I pushed the play button and ate pizza.

On the plus side, he did seem to enjoy the movie. When he finished eating, he carried his plate and used napkin to the kitchen. He was even nice enough to offer me another of my own beers.

When the movie ended I turned off the set, stood and led the way to the front door.

"Thanks, Miss Montoya," he said, at the door. "That was fun. Maybe we can do it again sometime."

"Are you out of your mind, Burke? I don't know you. I don't think I want to know you." I opened the door and stood to the side. "At least I know how you found me, being a cop. Thanks for returning the sweatshirt. Adios."

"Oh, come on," he said. "We got off on the wrong foot. Seriously. I would like to take you to dinner." Holding up a hand, he added, "or breakfast, and I know how that sounds. That's not what I meant."

"Thanks, but no thanks," I said, swinging the door open a little more. "I don't go out."

"Well, you do go to the beach once in a while," he corrected with another grin.

"Rarely," I said. "And probably not again. Bad experience at the beach."

"Then we have a slight problem, Miss Montoya."

"And that would be?"

"I'm the undercover cop assigned to your facility."

I stared at him. "Are you serious?"

"Yes, ma'am." At least he tried to look sheepish, although his eyes laughed. "Detective John Kincaid with the Monarch Beach Police Department can verify it for you. Or you can contact one of the other guys on the case. They're all gonna tell you the same thing. Agent Miller told you I was coming."

I closed my eyes, took in a gallon of air and sighed it back out. Sometimes you're the windshield, sometimes you're the bug. I was definitely doing bug time.

Opening my eyes I saw Burke patiently waiting for me to say something. With yet another sigh, I motioned him out the door.

"Come in the office tomorrow and I'll give you a code."

"Yes, ma'am," he smiled. "Thanks again for dinner. I'll see you in the morning."

"You paid for dinner," I countered.

I shut the door behind him and clicked the dead bolt as loudly as possible. I was pretty sure I heard him laugh as he went down the stairs.

Chapter 5

Sundays are usually slow at the facility, unless it's the tenth. A good day to get Burke set up.

I wasn't sure how I felt about this whole situation. His story sounded plausible although his methods left a lot to be desired. A whole lot.

Being smarter than the average bear, I called Agent Miller and verified Burke's story the first thing in the morning. He told the truth. Unless I filed a formal complaint, I was working with Declan Burke. My second call was to Steve, giving him an impromptu day off. If Burke was going to be incognito the fewer involved the better. Especially since Steve loved to talk.

Burke was waiting when I went downstairs. He climbed down from a big, shiny black pickup and waited while I opened the office.

Today he was wearing the uniform – local that is – of sweat shirt, jeans and sneakers. Unless it's hot, then it's a tee shirt and cargo shorts. Both require sneakers. He fit right in, could easily pass for a surfer or a fisherman. At least he wouldn't stick out like a neon sign flashing "COP".

I had him fill out an application like any other applicant while I made a pot of coffee. When it was ready I carried two cups out, setting one next to him on the counter. I went around and took my place at the computer.

"What should I fill in for employment history?" He pulled his coffee over and took a sip. "You want the truth or a polite lie?"

"With you, Burke, who knows the difference? I don't care what you put down."

"Are you going to be like that? Come on, lady, I'm trying here. I've explained, I've apologized and I'm trying to make this work."

With a sigh I leaned forward and looked at his application.

"This is fine," I said. "This is your code for access to the property," I added, handing him a slip of paper. "The gates are open from seven to seven for the regular customers, closed on all holidays. Your code is twenty four hours, so you can come in when you want. The only thing I ask is that you park out of sight if you're in after hours. I don't want to have to explain to the other customers. My official story is that you're the maintenance guy. The hired help. Most facilities hire couples so it's pretty common to have two people around."

He slid the little pink paper over, the one I had written his code on, looked at it for a couple of heartbeats. He reached up and took one of our business cards. He stuck the code on the back of the card before bringing out his wallet.

"No," I said.

He looked up at me. "What?"

"Don't put the code on my business card. You drop the card or lose it somewhere and you're giving someone twenty four hour access. Memorize it, or put it in your phone as a contact ID."

He pulled the code slip off the card and stuck it in his wallet, returning the business card to the holder on the counter. "Good point," he said. "Do you think that could have happened? That someone found a code to get them in?"

"It's possible," I said. "No matter how many times I explain it, people don't get it. They write 'storage code' on a slip and stick it to the dashboard of their car where anyone can see it. They put it on the refrigerator where all their friends can get it. All kinds of silly things. I literally picked up one of our cards in the parking lot at the grocery store and found a code written on the back, like you were going to do."

"What did you do?" he asked, leaning back and finishing his coffee.

"Shot him," I said, with a straight face.

He choked on his coffee and sprayed it down his shirt and across the counter. I slid his application out of the way and handed him the box of tissues I keep under the desk.

"I wouldn't be surprised," he said when he could. "Point taken, although the idea of you with a gun is scary enough."

"You might be surprised, Burke," I smiled.

He met my look. "Now what?"

"Now I show you around," I answered, standing up. "These are your keys. Please don't lay them down somewhere and forget them." Indicating the different colored rubber rings on the tops of the keys, I explained. "Red is for the overlocks, yellow is for company units, where most of the tools are kept. Blue is for the garage, where we keep the golf cart. The key to the cart is left in it, just remember to turn it off."

"What if someone steals the cart?"

"Then you chase them. You can probably catch them on foot. It's not that fast."

"Yes, ma'am."

"The other thing you need to know is the owners. They do come in from time to time. Mrs. Murphy has a couple of units here and her son has one of his own."

"Which son?"

I looked at Burke. "You know the sons?"

"I know most of the family. Paul and I went to school together."

"Then you'd recognize them if you run into them."

"Oh, yeah."

"How do we play that? Do they know you're a cop?"

He thought about it a minute. "Not positive but I don't think so. Haven't seen much of them the last few years. I've run into Paul a couple of times at the Gem but it was just a brief hello."

"Then it's up to you how to handle it," I said. "I report directly to Paul, indirectly to Mr. Murphy. I had to notify them of the undercover business, have them okay it. It is their business."

"Understandable. I think we'll be okay. What about Trick? Does he come in?"

I looked at him. "Who?"

"Trick. The younger son."

"Patrick?"

"Yeah," he said. "They always called him Trick. He had quite a way of dodging the ladies."

"I haven't met him. I've seen him on the cameras, helping his mom unload stuff. He's never introduced himself. Do you have a problem with him?"

"Nope. Doubt he'll remember me. He was a couple of years behind us, me and Paul. And we weren't that close. Played football, baseball, tennis, that stuff."

"School jocks?"

He chuckled. "You could say that. Mostly we competed. In everything."

"Academics?"

"Well, no, that was one area we left alone."

"As long as you know they can squelch this deal at any time. They have the right. I explained that to the DEA guy."

"Understood."

"Come on, let's go see the lot."

We spent an hour or so around the lot. I pointed out the company units where we stored ladders, hoses, garden tools, all the larger tools in one, another which held trash bags, light bulbs, sprayers and the other small tools. Burke asked a few questions and those he did ask were intelligent and to the point.

Being honest and observant I had to admit Declan Burke was a very good looking man and he appeared to be very fit. Wide shoulders, heavy chest and solid thighs. My guess would have been linebacker. If I had to guess. At least I wasn't going to have to worry about him not being in shape for the physical side of the lot, pretty sure he could manage a ladder and a broom without mishap.

I introduced him to the few customers in the lot when we were touring. He handled himself perfectly with just the right humility and graciousness, even joked with Randy, our resident spy.

Back in the office I took my seat behind the counter and checked the phone for any messages. Burke leaned on the counter.

"Anything else? Have I completed my training?"

"Looks like," I said. "If you need anything we don't have make me a list and I'll pick it up at the hardware store. We keep an open account at Greg's Hardware over in Monarch."

"Got it," he said. "Now am I through?"

"Far as I'm concerned," I said, leaning back in my chair.

"How about dinner tonight?"

I shook my head. "Sorry, not a good practice to hang out with the help."

He grinned at me. "We'll see," he said, before turning for the front door.

"When are you going to start," I called to his back.

"One day this week. Watch your cameras, you'll see me. Hard at work."

"Take care, then," I said, as he went out the front door.

He turned and shot me with finger and thumb. "You too, babe. See you soon."

I watched him go, heard him slam the door of his truck and then heard the engine kick over. This was going to be interesting.

~~~

I have to admit the guy worked his buns off over the next week. He was there when I came down to open the office on Monday morning, already at work in the back lot.

He had been sweeping for a while, to judge from the piles of sand and gravel lining the main corridor. Checking the cameras I saw several trash bags lined up along the first two buildings. He must have gotten an early start.

During the week he was in and out for several days - sweeping, bagging the trash, cleaning the driveways and along the fences. He would work for hours, disappear for a while, and come back before closing.

He went through the office several times a day, using the inside door to access the garage and the golf cart. Always a ready smile and some kind of innuendo on his way past the counter. A few times he came in for coffee in the morning, usually taking it with him.

I checked the camera recordings every morning but never saw him. If he was out there he was excellent at avoiding the cameras.

It was entertaining to watch him work. I noticed when it got hot in the afternoons he pulled off the sweatshirt, exposing a tee shirt tight across a broad chest, tight belly and narrow waist.

I wasn't the only one that noticed.

By Friday there was a marked increase in the female customer's visits during the late afternoon hours. Two in particular were in on Wednesday, Thursday and Friday. One of them brought him something on a covered plate and spent twenty minutes yakking at him.

Yes, I timed it.

She yapped while he leaned on his broom with one hand and balanced the plate with the other.

I watched on the video monitor, a technological peeping tom, wondering if he needed help. I was just about ready to go out and interrupt when she gave a little wave and sashayed back to her car. She wiggled like a plump pup all the way to her car. Excellent camera system. I could see her butt jiggle with every step she took.

By Friday I was glad to see the week end. Burke had finished sweeping the whole lot and cleaned along the fences, where plastic bags and trash often collect.

I had moments of guilt watching him work while I sat in the office. They passed quickly. He had the system down pat, knew what he was doing.

Closing time finally arrived and I headed upstairs as soon as I closed and locked the office. I went straight through to the bathroom and took a long shower. When I was finished I combed through my hair and left it loose. Pulling on some sweats I padded barefoot into the kitchen and put on the water for tea.

While I waited for the water to boil I hung on the refrigerator door and gazed inside. Grocery day was Saturday so the contents were bleak. Closing the door I went to the cupboards and understood how Old Mother Hubbard felt.

Pulling out a can of chicken soup, the standard make do meal for singles, I set it on the counter. I had just got down the tea bags when someone knocked on the door.

It is sadly common for a customer to arrive after the office has closed and assume, incorrectly, that I exist only to meet their needs. A sign at the bottom of the stairs clearly reads 'Private – Do No Bother Tenants'. I am always tempted to kick those who knock back down the stairs.

I snapped the door open, a hot rebuke already forming, to find Burke on the stairs, holding a huge brown paper bag.

"Hey, boss," he said. "How do you feel about Chinese food?"

Stuck on my own petard, my hunger overriding the company. I stepped back and held the door for him.

He came in and turned into the kitchen, setting the bag on the counter. "Didn't know what you like, so I got a variety," he said. "You want to get some plates?"

I moved next to him and pulled down a couple of plates. He was busy taking little white pasteboard containers out of the bag and setting them along the counter. The smells coming from them had me drooling.

I got down two glasses and filled them with ice while he finished spreading his feast. He rummaged in a drawer and found silverware while I poured tea into our glasses.

"A little bit of everything," he said, with a grin. "Chicken chow mein, fried rice, egg foo yung, sweet and sour pork, egg rolls and shrimp. If I missed anything we don't need it." He dumped out little packets of soy sauce and hot mustard before folding the bag and putting it beside the refrigerator. "Dig in," he said, still with that grin.

When it comes to food, I eat like a truck driver and have no modesty. I grabbed a spoon and began to fill my plate. Burke moved in right beside me and we bumped elbows getting a little of everything. Once the plates were loaded we each picked up a glass of iced tea and made our way to the couch.

Settled in, I handed him the remote. "You brought dinner, you get the controls," I said. "And thank you. This is perfect."

He turned on the television. "Glad you like Chinese. What channel is the movie channel?"

I couldn't help it, I chuckled. "Make yourself at home, Burke. They start at 225. The oldies are on 237."

"Why are you laughing? I brought food."

"Yes, you did. And I thanked you."

"How about W.C. Fields?"

"Love him," I said around a mouth full of egg roll.

With that we sat back side by side, eating Chinese food and laughing at the old black and white film. Almost eighty years later it was still funny.

It was almost ten o'clock by the time the movie ended. I boxed up leftovers for him to take but he refused.

"I'm staying in my motor home right now," he explained. "Not much room in my fridge. You keep them. If I get hungry I can always come up here."

"Hardly. You can however go into the break room downstairs. I'll take them down in the morning and leave them in the fridge."

"Spoilsport," he grinned, leaning back against the counter.

"Thanks for dinner, Burke," I said, leading the way to the front door. "Have a good night."

I opened the front door for him, stepping back so he could leave. He caught me by the shoulders, dropped his head and planted a quick kiss on my lips. "Thanks, babe. I hate to eat alone."

He was three stairs down and moving by the time I blinked. At the bottom of the stairs he turned to look up at me. His eyes glinted in the light of the porch lamp. "I haven't forgotten that kiss," he said softly. "I'm working my way up to it."

"Gonna take more than Chinese food," I called back and shut the door. With my own smile I twisted the lock and shot the dead bolt.

Chapter 6

Over the next two weeks we settled into a pattern.

Burke checked in two or three days a week, picking up a list of things to do and a cup of coffee before going to work in the lot. Those days he usually stayed for dinner – whether we ordered out or I cooked.

We usually followed dinner with a movie, the evening stretching to ten or so before Burke headed home, wherever that was.

Several times I noticed that fresh, outdoor smell on his clothes when he came to the office in the morning, that same smell that was on my sweatshirt when it was returned.

He laughed when I asked about it, and explained that he was currently living out of his motor home. He had a small washing machine but relied on a clothes line to dry his laundry. He did give me points for picking up on the scent.

We were comfortable together, sharing many of the same tastes – food and movies. When it came to sports, specifically the NFL, we went our separate ways. I am, and have been, a fan of the Dallas Cowboys while he roots for the San Francisco Forty-Niners. Mortal enemies.

The nine cartons of drugs remained untouched.

In Burke's case, someone could have lit up a pipe in his truck and he wouldn't even blink. He was still undercover, had been for close to two years, gathering info, following leads. While he never shared inside information he did teach me a little about the drug pipeline.

We have hundreds of miles of coastline in California, most of it accessible from the sea. Our local news often reports an empty Panga boat floating in the surf or run up on the beach or rocks.

I asked Burke about that and he explained they are a common fishing boat, with a high bow and a wide center, light enough to be powered by a couple of good outboard motors.

Loaded with drugs they can run at night, follow along the coast and layup when necessary with a common GPS system. Hard to see close to shore, easy to handle, and fast.

A pre-arranged meeting point, a rental truck, a quick off load and it's off again, innocent fisherman if stopped. Easy to abandon when necessary. Pull the motors off and load them in the truck with the cargo and off you go, leaving the boat behind. In some cases even the outboard motors were abandoned.

Considering the amount of drugs they can carry in a shipment, the cost of the boat never enters the equation.

Jade Beach is located about half way between Los Angeles and San Francisco, convenient for shipments going either way. There's also the great central valley that runs right through the center of the state only three hours east.

Burke referred to our area as a hub – convenient place to load up and move out, in any of three different directions. In past months he had been active in San

Diego, before moving up to Los Angeles and now here, traveling among and with different drug dealers, infiltrating and working to find the main source.

There were days in a row that Burke failed to appear, followed by a chain of days where he could be found actively working in the lot.

I did have to caution him about taking off his shirt, which amused him no end. He was, after all, undercover and supposed to be unobtrusive. Fawning females spending hours at a time in small talk brought him a lot of attention.

He insisted I was jealous, and while I hotly disagreed, he wasn't far off base. The blond hair, dark eyes, and rugged build fit together nicely and I wasn't dead.

We settled into a comfortable arrangement – dinner two or three nights a week, movies, football games – an easy, laid back relationship with no stress or strain. He was an excellent companion, knowledgeable on many things, well read, and had a great sense of humor. I've always been up for a laugh.

If he was there, fine.

If not? Also fine.

The first of the month drew close and things got busy. Customers moving out of units, new rentals moving in, traffic in and out of the office with rent payments.

While many customers were billed automatically on their credit cards others chose to come in and pay in person.

Somewhere in the last three days of the month the nine cartons of drugs disappeared.

On a whim, during a late night drive the last day of the month, I removed the yellow snap tag and went inside to check the cartons.

They were gone.

I spent hours reviewing video, checking each camera back several days, monitoring the activity around the unit. I was up till one or two in the morning, monitoring the hard copies of access sheets the past couple of weeks. I wondered if Burke had moved them.

A lot of lost sleep and too much caffeine left me with a few leads.

There were three different pickup trucks with shells on the back, six rental trucks, and four vans around the unit blocking a clear view of the unit door, not to mention the various cars back and forth in the aisle. That was just the past week.

I found nothing I could pin down.

When Burke returned he took copies of everything and backtracked everything I had done. Burke found nothing.

He explained he had been on another case for three days. The bodies of two men had been dumped near the freeway, both shot in the back of the head. One was a known drug dealer identified by Agent Miller. Burke was called in to work that case.

In his absence, right under my nose, the drugs had been removed.

~~~~

The fifth of the month Detective John Kincaid wandered into the office again. I spotted the wide shoulders and sun touched hair coming across the parking lot.

He waited politely while I finished up with a customer.

"Miss Montoya," he greeted, once the customer was gone. "How are things going here?"

"Same old thing, different day, Detective. What can I do for you?"

"John, remember?"

"John," I said. "What can I do for you today?"

Kincaid did a slow look around the office, settling on the video monitor behind me.

"I hear we lost the drugs."

"Yes, sir. John."

"Relax, ma'am," he grinned. "I'm only following up. Trying to stay in the loop. I gather you didn't see anything?"

"No, sorry. I've reviewed all the video, all the hard copies. Nada."

"The undercover guy didn't see anything either?"

"Nope. Burke wasn't on site. His schedule is random and he was called away for a few days."

Kincaid looked up at me. "Burke?"

"The California CID guy. His name is Burke."

"Haven't met him," the detective admitted. "Maybe I better introduce myself."

I glanced over at the monitor. "He's not back there right now. I can ask him to call you."

"No need. I'll catch up with him. Couple of questions?"

"Shoot," I said.

"Is anyone on duty during the night? Someone on the lot?"

"No, sir. The security cameras run twenty-four seven. They have infrared filters for evening hours. I have the same software on my computer upstairs, so I can check randomly. Any camera. Not a regular schedule, although always before I go to bed. Any movement at all I would notice."

He nodded. "This Burke is only here during the day?"

"Yes, sir."

"John."

"John," I corrected. "There are times he's here after hours, just not out in the lot."

Kincaid's eyebrow rose. "He's here? In the office? Does he watch the cameras?"

Oh, boy. "No. He has dinner here once in a while."

"Oh, I see. He brings his dinner and watches the camera's while he eats. Good idea. Fresh eyes, different perspective."

I thought about it for a second. "He often has dinner with me. Upstairs."

The eyebrow rose again. "Personal?"

"Not the way you obviously think. No. We work together quite a bit. We're friends. We split a pizza, watch a movie, sometimes a couple of beers."

"Also understandable. I wasn't trying to pry." He smiled at me.

"Nothing to hide," I said, returning his smile. "We work together. Have a lot of things in common. That's it."

He straightened up and double patted the counter with his hands.

"Okay, then. Just checking in with you. If you think of anything, or see anything, give me a call. I assume you know not to approach anyone. I'm only a few minutes away."

"I have enough sense not to confront suspected drug dealers," I smiled.

"Good to know," he smiled back. "You have my card."

"Yes, I do. Right here in the drawer."

"Okay then. I'll check back."

"Anytime," I said.

He tossed me a little salute and left. I watched him climb in his truck and drive away, feeling somehow I had let him down.

Determined to come up with something, I burned DVD's of those trucks and vans I had marked and took them upstairs with me when the office closed.

After a grilled cheese sandwich and a can of soup, I made a pot of coffee and settled on the couch with my laptop.

Frame by frame, camera by camera, I went back over the images.

Close to midnight, I saw something.

Or thought I did.

I checked the time stamps on the camera recordings to the hard copy pages of the log in sheets.

The rental truck, a popular name, logged in on a six hundred code as close as I could figure. The truck was parked in front of the four hundred building. The two buildings bracketed the same aisle, across from each other, the drive being wide enough for another vehicle to pass one parked there.

A dark blue van pulled up beside the rental, effectively blocking the aisle for a short period, nine minutes in all. Long enough that I would have gone out and had one of them move if I had noticed.

Eleven minutes later the same van pulled into the same place, beside the rental truck, going the other direction. This time, just briefly, the driver's face was visible.

I backed up the image and double checked the printout.

No one had logged out in those eleven minutes.

For some reason, the van had moved out of camera range, then returned eleven minutes later.

I froze the frame with the driver's face and printed it out.

Blurry, yes, but a thread. The driver appeared to be dark complected, a thin mustache and a soul patch on his bottom lip, long hair topped with a baseball cap shadowing his eyes.

He climbed out of the truck, walked back to check a tire, or the gas tank door, something his body blocked from sight. Two minutes. Then he went back to the cab, looked around for just a second or two, and climbed in. Another minute. He started the truck and pulled out, disappearing from range.

I looked down at my notes, wondering if I had found something.

My eyes burned from the late hours, staring at the screen, so I called it a night. Shutting down the computer, I cleaned up my dishes and cleared the table, scooping the printed photo, the logs and my notes into a pile. I slipped the thin stack into a folder and stuck it under the coffee table, to be filed tomorrow.

Checking the lot one last time, I ran through the live camera's one at a time. Nothing moved, nothing changed. Everything quiet and normal.

I shut everything down and went to bed.

Chapter 7

The rest of the week was busy, with the rents all due and a few empties to clean and rent. Burke was still absent so the cleaning duties all fell to me. Once the office was closed, it was roll out the cart and start getting the units ready to rent.

I doubled the time I spent cruising the lot after hours, hoping to see something, anything that would give me an idea. Wasted effort. Nothing out of the ordinary.

On Thursday I locked up in time to pick up chicken tacos from the Mexican restaurant before the football game started. Back at home I pulled on sweats, grabbed my dinner and parked in front of the television, just after kickoff. Neither of the teams was a favorite but it was football and I needed a break.

Sure enough, the missing Burke showed up before the first quarter ended. He looked rough – unshaven, circles under his eyes, and a general worn out expression. Not the usual perky, upbeat smart ass I was accustomed to.

"Didn't expect you, so I already ate," I said, standing aside for him to come on in. "There's ham or peanut butter if you want a sandwich."

He dropped wearily onto the couch and dropped his head back, closing his eyes.

"Not even hungry," he said from that position. "Just glad to be home."

I resumed my seat and picked up my beer.

"I have beer or soda," I said, my eyes going back to the screen.

"I'll get something in a minute," he said softly.

I left him alone, a little concerned that he considered this 'home'. We might have to talk about that. He was a good companion, fun to be with and I enjoyed his company. Home? Not happening.

I finished my beer in silence.

At half time I picked up my mess and took it to the kitchen.

When I turned around to go back in the living room Burke was there, close behind me. Without a word he gathered me in his arms and pulled me against his chest. My hands automatically went around him and we stood there for several minutes, sort of rocking back and forth and holding each other.

He rubbed his cheek against mine and then I felt his lips on my neck.

I stepped back and dropped my arms.

Looking at him, his eyes shadowed, looking almost bruised, I couldn't read his expression, or his intention. I enjoyed his company but I was not about to climb in the sack with him.

After a long moment he seemed to reach the same conclusion and stepped back, giving me a lot more room. He shook his head a couple of times and looked back at me.

"Sorry, Marlena, just so damned tired."

"Want me to make some coffee? Fix you some eggs?"

"Sounds good. The eggs. Not the coffee. Maybe some toast? Milk? I've had enough coffee to float a battleship."

"Sure, no problem. You go sit down and I'll get it together."

With a deep sigh he turned around and went back to the living room while I pulled out a carton of eggs.

I scrambled a couple of eggs with some cheese, buttered a couple of slices of toast and carried the plate and a glass of milk into the living room.

Burke was sound asleep, slumped into a corner of the couch, his feet still on the floor.

I set the plate and milk on the table and looked at the man on my couch.

After a minute I picked up the stuff and took it back to the kitchen. Returning I grabbed a blanket off my bed and covered Burke, after first removing his shoes and lifting his legs up to the couch.

He groaned once, and stretched out a little bit but never actually woke up.

I locked up and turned off the lights, leaving the light over the stove on in case Burke woke up disoriented. I turned off the television and went to brush my teeth.

In bed I picked up my Kindle and read for a while. When I turned off the light I could hear Burke snoring in the other room. I drifted off to sleep listening to him, surprised at how comforting the sound was.

He was still sleeping the next morning, having turned over and pulled the blanket close. He looked a lot younger relaxed like that.

I started the coffee, grabbed some clothes and went to the bathroom, not wanting to get caught dressing.

Drying off after my shower I thought I heard voices. Maybe Burke had turned on the television. I dressed quickly and hurried out to the living room, the smell of fresh coffee filling the room.

My boss, one of them anyway, Paul Murphy sat on my couch holding a cup of coffee. Burke sat in my chair likewise armed with coffee.

"Good morning," I said, moving straight to the kitchen.

"Good morning," Paul replied.

"Morning, babe," Burke said as I passed him. "Coffee's ready."

Of course the coffee is ready, I started it before my shower. I poured a cup, added milk, and listened to the silence in my living room.

"Paul is here," Burke said, coming around the corner. "Why don't you talk to him and I'll get some breakfast going."

I gave Burke a look that should have frozen him to floor and went around him.

"What can I do for you, Paul?" I asked, claiming my chair.

Paul is another big guy, reported to be quite a player around town, and in his eyes I could read exactly what he thought he knew. There was a sparkle, a glint I had never seen before. Preferring not to draw even more attention to the situation by trying to explain, I tried to look unconcerned. Not easy when I would prefer to kick Burke down the stairs and count how many he hit on the way down.

"I didn't mean to interrupt," Paul began, with a knowing little grin. "The office wasn't open and I wanted to check with you about the drug guys."

I interrupted. "The office opens at nine," I told him. "It's only eight."

"Right, okay, then," he was still smirking at me. I wanted to slap him and fortunately thought better of it.

He settled back in the couch cushions and sipped from his cup.

"As far as the 'drug guys' go, that's your man right there. Ask him."

Paul leaned forward and shook his pony tail back over his shoulder, finishing his coffee and setting the cup down.

"Well, he didn't have much to offer," he said with a grin. "I woke him up."

I counted to ten and took a deep breath.

"I emailed a report," I began. "The drugs went missing. No idea how. I've triple checked all our cameras and logs. Could have been one of maybe a dozen people. It's even possible they somehow got past the cameras during the night, but I doubt that one. I sent Agent Miller the same report I sent to you."

"So we got nothing," Paul said.

"Yes, sir. That's about it."

Burke had come back, taking a stance behind my chair.

Paul looked at him. "So, it's no help for you to be here. A waste of time."

"He's got a lot of work done," I interrupted. "Repaired units, cleaned up."

Paul's eyes shot to me. "We don't pay him to maintain this place. Is it getting to be too much for you? Should we be looking for another manager?"

My temper flashed and I bit down on the inside of my cheek to stop my first response.

"My understanding is that I could hire any help I needed, to offset being single. I haven't hired anyone. I've done it myself and the facility is doing very well. Burke has done the work around here as part of the undercover project."

"Whoa, don't get huffy with me," Paul responded. "I'm just asking. I am the owner. I have the right to know what's happening on my property."

I sighed. "Yes, sir, you're right. I've kept you in the loop with weekly reports. I don't know what else I can tell you. Perhaps you could check with Agent Miller or Detective Kincaid. Their numbers are in my reports. They may have more information than I do."

Burke stepped around my chair to face Paul.

"I've been out of town," he told the other man. "I will get in touch with the Bureau and see if they've learned anything new, but I sincerely doubt it. No one is to blame for those drugs going missing. I've looked at the tapes, checked the whole lot. I disagree that there's no need for me to be here. They came back. Whoever it is, came back to retrieve those drugs."

"Hell yes they did," Paul said. "That was a lot of money."

Burke cocked an eyebrow at him. "You know that for a fact?"

Paul looked uncomfortable for a second, just a flash of red in his cheeks. "Just from reading and seeing the

64

news. Anyone can figure out that nine boxes of drugs is a lot of money."

"Agreed," Burke said. "Enough that someone came back for them."

"So they're gone. No need for you to hang around."

Burke chuckled and shook his head. "You want me to rent a unit, Paul? That make you feel better?"

Paul stood up. "That has nothing to do with it, Burke. I don't care if you move in here. Looks like you already have." He smirked at me.

"Hang on," I said, standing too. "Burke was here late, and fell asleep on the couch."

"I don't care," Paul interrupted again. "No skin off my nose. What I am saying is that I have someone on my property that doesn't belong here. If the drugs are gone, he doesn't need to here."

"That bother you? Me being on the property? You have something to hide?" Burke went on the attack, his eyes hard, the muscles in his jaw clenching.

"Not a damn thing," Paul answered with a shrug. "State wants to pay you to loaf around I got no problem with it. Just don't see a need for it. And I'll tell the old man that, too."

That sounded like a threat.

"I disagree," Burke countered. "You don't get it. Someone put the drugs here. Was that the first time? Have they been using this place all along? We don't know. Yet. We do know they came back. They may not know we're onto the plan. There is a possibility they'll stay with the system. If I can shut down a limb of this tree, we all benefit. It's worth a shot. What's to lose?"

"I'll talk to the old man, see what he says," Paul said. He eased around the coffee table and went towards the front door. Burke stepped back and let him go.

"I can talk to your dad," Burke said. "I really feel like this could be a break."

Paul looked at me, and then at Burke. "All right. Give it another couple of weeks. Then we'll get together and see where to go from there."

"Fair enough," Burke said, holding out his hand. "It's good to see you again, Paul."

Paul shook hands and opened the door. "Enjoy the rest of your day," he said on his way out, winking at me.

"We will," Burke answered, and closed the door behind him.

"Here's another fine mess you've gotten me into," I told him, when Paul's footsteps faded down the stairs.

Burke grinned at me.

"He's just jealous," he chuckled. "Always has been."

"Nothing for him to be jealous of," I corrected. "You know what happened as well as I do."

"He doesn't know that," Burke laughed. "I love getting his goat. Keeps him on his toes."

"And he's gonna get on my toes," I said, getting up and going to the kitchen. "I guarantee that is not going to go over well."

"Ah, come on, Marlena," Burke argued, coming to fill his cup again. "No harm done. It's not like you have someone else. Even your boss can't tell you who you can date."

He was right. Didn't help. I was still ticked off.

"You're up, you're dressed, you're out of here," I told him, turning my back.

"Come on, babe. Not even breakfast? I already cooked the bacon."

I counted to ten again, then turned and leaned back against the counter. "You've done enough damage today. Go to work. You can buy breakfast at Kelly's or hit the drive through."

Burke sighed and set his cup down. He needed a shave, his thick blond hair was flattened on one side, and his shirt wrinkled in fifty places, still better than he had looked when he rolled in last night. The circles under his eyes weren't as dark nor as puffy.

"Thanks for the couch," he mumbled, heading for the door.

"You're welcome," I said, and left it at that.

He gave me a long, searching look before he finally opened the door and closed it behind him.

I opened the office and promptly checked all the cameras to be sure Paul Murphy was off the premises. Once I was sure he was absent, I put on another pot of coffee and went to work.

With the events of the morning, I had forgotten to show Burke the picture I had printed off. Coming out of the shower, dressed and ready for coffee to find your boss on the couch is not a good start on the day.

I brought the file down at lunch and went over it again, seeing nothing new. I stuck it under the counter to give to Burke the next time I saw him. Whenever that would be.

I just finished that thought when he walked in.

He looked a whole lot better than he had this morning, having shaved and cleaned up. A white collar peeked over a green sweater worn over jeans. He looked a little sheepish.

I waited, giving him the lead.

He glanced around the office, folded his arms and leaned on the counter.

"Are we speaking?"

"Of course. Can I help you?"

Burke chuckled. "How about I say I'm sorry? Really, all I did was open the door. You were in the shower. It could have been a customer, you know. What if someone was stuck at the gate? Or a door fell? I mean, after all, the customers know me, I've been around for a while. If it was an emergency I could have handled it."

Valid points all. He could indeed have handled almost anything, including opening the office if need be. He had keys. There was no way he could have known Paul would come by the apartment. That in itself was unusual. None of the Murphy clan ever came to my living quarters, not even when I was hired. The previous manager had shown me around.

"Apology accepted," I told him. "It really wasn't your fault."

"Thank you," Burke smiled, and moved around to take a seat at the counter. "Now, how about dinner? Let me take you out for a change."

I thought about it. "I don't think so," I said.

"Afraid to be seen with me? It's just dinner. At Kelly's," he added naming the diner in Monarch that was everyone's favorite place to eat. "It's Thursday, chicken and dumplings. I'll even spring for dessert."

He looked so sincere, batting his lashes at me while trying not to grin.

"Fine," I said. "Let me get locked up."

He straightened up and went to flip the signs around to Closed. "I'll help."

On our way out I grabbed the folder from under the counter.

Chapter 8

Kelly's is a diner, a casual place with the best food in the county and the best prices. Always reasonable, always tasty, and almost always leftovers to be brought home and reheated later. If you're not too late they have wonderful pies from the local bakery.

We drove in Burke's truck, a newer model with all the bells and whistles, exchanging small talk. He asked about the folder I had placed on the seat.

"Something for you to look at later," I explained. "I finally found a frame with a partial look at the driver of the Move It truck. Thought maybe you might recognize him although it's not the best copy in the world."

"I'll look at it tonight," he said. "Anything else come up?"

"Not that I can see," I answered. "It must be happening at night. Somehow they're getting in and avoiding the cameras. Only other way is careful planning, using someone else to block the view. That would be tricky."

"The thing is," Burke began, turning into Kelly's parking lot, "that storage unit is not important."

"What do you mean?"

"Think about it, babe. That was only nine cartons. A lot of drugs, granted, but not a full load. Were there more? And where were they? That unit was empty, right? Before they put those cartons in?"

"Yes. It was supposed to be. It had one of the little yellow snap tags on the door. I put that on myself."

He turned off the truck and angled towards me. "I think that was leftovers or extras, that they had filled another unit somewhere close and didn't have enough room for those last boxes. Or maybe someone interrupted them and they had to dump them off quick. The rest of the load was delivered on schedule, wherever that was. I think they came back to see if those nine were still there, and when they were? They took them."

"So you think another unit is being used to store the drugs. Couldn't a dog find it?"

Burke sighed deeply and turned back around. "Dogs could find the truck. Not necessarily the unit. Depends on so many things. So many scents can camouflage the smell of drugs. Coffee, cinnamon, even vanilla can override the scent. Plus, that was careful packaging. The plastic bags, inside a plastic covered carton and wrapped in more plastic. Not a lot of smell coming through all that. Come on, let's eat. I'll look at the picture later. Let's just get away from it all for a while."

He stepped down from the truck and jogged around to open my door.

Not accustomed to such actions I had already popped the door and started to step down. Burke caught my arm and held it till I was on my feet.

"Sorry," I murmured, "not used to help."

"You don't need help, babe, I know that. My mama just raised me to be polite to women. All women."

Glancing at him I could see his grin in the dim light of the parking lot.

"Come on," he said, taking my arm again, "let's go eat."

We had a nice dinner, both of us ordering the chicken and dumplings, which came with a side salad, and iced tea.

We exchanged small talk while we ate, nothing about the case or the events of the morning, dwelling mostly on old movies and a book Burke had just finished and recommended to me.

He paid and we left, me with a Styrofoam box of leftovers.

When we were back at the facility Burke wanted to take a drive through. I opted to be dropped off at the gate.

Instead Burke turned in and parked at the bottom of the stairs.

Turning off the engine, he reached for the door handle. "Stay," he said, and hopped out to come around and open my door for me.

"This isn't necessary," I told him as he helped me down from the truck. "You could have just dropped me off. Go take a look around. I can manage the stairs just fine."

Burke tugged the arm he was holding and drew me close. "I asked you out. That is a form of a date, like it or not. I will see you to your door."

"Mama again?"

He laughed out loud, and hugged me against his side. "Yep, that's it. She would shoot me if I just dropped you at the gate."

I leaned against him for a minute, careful to keep my box of leftovers to the side. "Does your mom live close by?"

He let me go quickly and stepped back, guiding me towards the stairs with a hand on my back. "She's dead," he said flatly. "Years ago."

"Oh, I'm so sorry!" He had never mentioned family and I felt rather foolish.

"No need. Long time ago." He glanced at me and his look softened. "You didn't know."

I led the way upstairs and unlocked the door. Burke followed me in, closing the door behind him. While I put the leftovers in the fridge he took a seat on the couch, leaning his head back and closing his eyes. Déjà vu.

"If you're that tired you better head home."

He sat up and rubbed the back of his neck. "Is that a request? Or an order?"

"Take it any way you choose. Thank you for dinner." I remained standing.

He took the hint and stood up, pulling his keys from his pocket.

"You're welcome, Marlena. I enjoyed it. Hope we can do it again." He was moving for the door as he talked and I followed a step behind him. At the door he paused and turned back to me, darting in and giving me a quick kiss. "Thanks for going with me."

"I had a good time, too," I said, easing back a step. "You be in tomorrow?"

He smiled and stepped outside. "Yes, boss. I'll be here."

I stood in the open door and watched him down the stairs. "Take a look at that file," I called after him. "I left it on the seat."

He waved a hand over his shoulder. "Will do. Good night."

"Good night, Burke. Thanks again for dinner."

He waved again and drifted into the dark at the bottom of the stairs.

I locked up behind him.

True to his word, he was on the lot when I opened the office the following morning. I could see the golf cart parked near Building 3 although he wasn't in sight. I went in and started the coffee, figuring he would be in shortly.

By the time the coffee finished he came in looking much better than the last few days. He was flushed from the sun or the effort, putting some color in his freshly shaved face. His eyes were bright and clear.

"Good morning," I said when he came in, handing him a cup of coffee. "You started early."

"Yes, ma'am. Wanted to get after it." He pulled out a chair and sat down. "Got an idea I wanted to run past you." He paused long enough to sip coffee.

"Go ahead," I told him, lifting my own cup.

"That space along the fence, in the back, space 29."

I nodded.

"How about I bring my motor home down here, park in that space? I can watch the place from there, give us another perspective. Maybe see something at night. What do you think?"

I thought about it for a minute and nodded again. "Up to you. I don't think the Murphy's will care, although I will have to clear it with Paul or Papa Murphy."

Burke scoffed. "You don't need to worry about me. What can happen? I fall down the steps to the motor home? Just thought it might be a good idea, be around here at night."

"I'll clear it with the Murphys. Get back to you as soon as I know something. Do you really think it will help?"

Burke took in a few gallons of air and blew it out loudly. "I don't know," he said finally. "I'm running out of ideas. I've been on this thing so long I don't know what to do. It's one dead end after another."

"Do you really think this is a regular deal? Them using my facility to store drugs?"

"Store? No, I don't think so. That's too static, too easy to stumble across. Do I think it may be a regular drop off point? Yes. Sadly, I do. If you think about it, perfect place to change loads. Boat comes in late at night, gets unloaded into a rental truck of some kind. Or even a moving van, hell, a turnip truck! Something. Say you're running late, or daylight rolls around, whatever. You need a place to split up the cargo, someplace to store it till someone else can pick up their half. You can't just park on the side of the road, Marlena. You don't want to draw attention to it, you know? What better place than a storage yard? In this area of the state there's not a lot of big warehouses, like a big furniture warehouse or a big materials warehouse. The large buildings in Jade are filled with boats or boat parts."

I thought about what he said. We don't have any major businesses or chains around here. One of the reasons so many of our young people move on is the lack of jobs. Oh, sure, you can flip burgers or work on the docks, help on a fishing boat. There's just nothing to make a career. No towering levels of high tech businesses humming along broad boulevards lined with brand name coffee shops. Not here. Not even close.

About the only place readily available to store anything is a storage facility. And Beach Storage was the only one in the area, unless you counted the boat storage yards in Jade and most of those are outdoors.

"Couldn't you unload into a boat? Another boat? Like in the boat yards? There's all kinds of boats stored there, acres of 'em. Some are pretty good size. At least as big as a Move It rental truck."

"That could work, babe. Couple things wrong. You're unloading a truck into a boat, the boat up on blocks, or a crane so you're spending a lot more time out in the open to get the boxes out of the truck and onto the boat. Plus, why would anyone be loading cartons into a beached boat? That's gonna make people way curious. I know it would make me curious, even if I was just a mechanic."

I took my turn at sighing. Covered trucks, box vans, all are common sights at any storage facility, some of them even rent the moving trucks.

I know there's three major companies with storage in my lot – like Bake It Right, the cakes and cookies people. Their products are in all the grocery stores, liquor stores, even the high school. Their big sixteen wheeler comes in every Monday, pulls up to their unit and rolls a ramp out the side door and starts filling up the unit. After that their local man comes in with a smaller van, loads up what he needs and begins his route, delivering all over our area and Monarch Beach next door. He works every day but Sunday. Monday it starts all over again.

We're sort of the distribution center. What works for cupcakes could work for drugs.

Was there a chance one of my favorite customers was running drugs? That thought upset me a little. How well did I really know these people? Hardly at all. I knew more about T. Tom Tanner from magazines than from him personally.

The Bake It Right driver came in from Arizona every week. He had mentioned the drive several times, how early they had to get up, the weather between home and here. He had mentioned stops in Los Angeles and Santa Barbara at different times.

I had been by when they were unloading, the cartons rolling quickly down the steel conveyor belt to be stacked in the unit. I couldn't swear in court what was inside those cartons. They were a nationwide company, had been for years, and I was pretty sure they made enough off their bakery line that they didn't need to dabble in drugs.

Still, it underlined how easy it would be to store and distribute drugs from my facility. The major problem I faced was finding out if and who.

"Penny for your thoughts," Burke interrupted.

"Lot to take in," I said. "Put like that, it could be anyone. Well, anyone with a van or truck."

"Exactly," Burke agreed. "It's a big ball of string, babe. If I can find a loose end the whole thing will unravel. It's finding that loose end. And there's always the chance they moved on."

"And how do we know?"

Burke sighed again and stood up. "Gonna start by getting my motor home in here. If the boss says okay." He pushed his chair in and looked at me. "How about pizza and a movie tonight? I'll buy the pizza, you pick the movie."

"Sounds good," I said. "I'll call Papa Murphy right now."

"Thanks. Let me know," he called over his shoulder on his way out.

After Burke left I went around Paul by calling Papa Murphy and getting his permission to move in the motor home. Asking Paul for permission to have Burke living here, even temporarily, was not something I wanted to do. He had the wrong impression already. Why add to it?

When Burke came in around lunch time I told him he could bring in the motor home. He thanked me and reminded me we had dinner plans before once again taking off.

I spent the afternoon going over the customer list.

Being blessed with an excellent memory has its drawbacks. More than four hundred customers were listed. Some were couples or families and I could remember a lot of them. The stinkers rose to the top like helium balloons, followed by the long timers, those who had been here the longest. No way could I recall them all.

A handful were here longer than me. Could I reasonably eliminate them due to longevity? The only people I could actually eliminate were the owners – Mr. and Mrs. Murphy, Paul and his wife, who came in at times, and Patrick, who only visited the site when helping his mom.

The only other customer I could eliminate was Randy. He was from a different generation where integrity and honor were highly valued and a man was as good as his word.

I knew I didn't have anything to do with it so that pared down the list of suspects. By about seven. It's a start. Maybe Burke had the right idea with the motor home. The dark hours might hold some answers.

About an hour before closing Burke rolled in, literally.

The motor home was beige with brown striping and looked about twenty five feet long.

He had to climb down to enter his code, then hop back up, shut the door and get through the gate before it closed. I found it entertaining to watch him hop around, since I could have just pushed a button in the office and opened the gate for him.

I watched the cameras to see him pull in and park along the back fence. Some customers have to back and forth a dozen times to get situated. Burke did it the first time, pulling head in rather than backing like most. A wide tinted window split the rear of the vehicle when it was in position, giving the tenant an excellent view. In this case the view encompassed the rear aisle around the buildings as well as the west side of the facility.

He was still inside when I closed the office and locked up for the day.

~~~

I took a quick shower, pulled on my sweats and turned on the television to look for a movie. The local news was on with the weather so I hesitated to get the forecast. The weather guy did the report then told us to stay tuned for the latest on the double murder in Jade Beach. I didn't know there was a double murder in Jade Beach, so I waited through a half dozen commercials.

The update the anchor promised amounted to nothing, just saying there was nothing new in the search for whoever killed two young Latino men found dumped near the freeway. I was ready to change channels when they showed pictures of the two men in better days.

The one on the right was identified as Carlos Reynaldo Esquibel. I didn't even look at the second guy. I focused on Carlos. He looked familiar. He looked a lot like the picture I had copied from the office tapes. I hit the pause button and went to get the folder.

By the time Burke showed up with dinner I was pretty sure this was the same guy. The television was playing Pong with the station logo so I could hold the image of Mr. Esquibel. I already recorded the segment in case I needed it later.

Burke knocked and came in, going directly to the kitchen with a square box. He called out from around the corner "you want beer or soda?"

"Beer, please," I answered. "Come look at this."

"Can I get dinner first? I'm starved."

With a sigh I got up to help him. He had the paper plates and napkins in hand so I grabbed a beer and a soda and followed him back to the living room.

He sat in his usual place on the couch before looking at the tv. "What am I looking at?" he asked.

"I saw this on the news," I explained. "I saved it for you."

"What is it? I'm hungry."

"Just watch it," I said.

The piece was about five minutes and when it finished, I rewound it in case Burke wanted to see it again.

"And?"

I was disappointed he didn't see it right away. "That guy! He looks like the same guy on the tape. The one I gave you, remember? When the drugs were taken? I burned you a copy. This is the guy coming around the corner of that truck!"

Burke gave me a glance, chewed pizza and looked at the screen. "Back it up," he said. "Let's see it again."

Happy with my clue and the attention he was giving it I rewound and showed it again.

"I don't get it," he said when the news clip had played through. "What am I looking at?"

"That guy," I said, pointing at the screen. "That's the same guy. The one on my tape." I rewound and played it again. "See? Right there. On the right."

Burke chewed and looked again at the screen. "I don't see it, babe. The guy you taped here was heavier and older. Sorry."

I sat back with a thud, disappointed. "You don't see it?"

"I don't think they're the same. Maybe a slight resemblance because of the hair and the soul patch. Otherwise? Uh – uh. I was called in on the homicide, babe. I saw those bodies up close and I'm telling you not the same guy."

"You're on this case, too?"

"Not officially. I was called in to see if I could identify either one of them. Maybe one of the dealers I've dealt with or seen around. Nada. Never saw these guys before. Or your guy out back. Now, what movie did you get?"

Okay, I sulked. I was proud of my clue. To hear him poo-poo it ticked me off.

"I didn't get one," I said. "I was side tracked."

Burke took a deep breath and sighed it out, setting his slice of pizza down. "Come on, Marlena," he said, patting my knee. "It was close. I admit it. If I hadn't seen him up close I might have made the same mistake. You did a good job, a great job. Proves you're on your toes, a regular part of the team. If you'll feel better, I'll pass it on to the task force. Just don't be disappointed when it gets tossed. Okay?"

With my own sigh I agreed and handed him the remote. "You find a movie. I'll get the napkins."

Chapter 9

Burke stayed in his motor home the next three nights, leaving his pickup parked down the block and walking in before the gates locked. I checked the cameras often and never saw him. If he was wandering the property he did an excellent job of avoiding the camera system.

I kept my file with the picture I had printed out. On Friday I bought the local paper to see if they printed the pictures of the murdered men. No such luck. I could find every yard sale in the county but nothing about the two men. Small town, weekly paper.

My disappointment carried me through the day. When Burke failed to show I decided to get away from it all and treat myself to dinner Kelly's. Fish and chips sounded pretty good. Not cooking sounded even better.

I found a seat at the counter and placed my order, adding a salad and iced tea. The waitress brought the salad and tea and smiled at me. "Thank God it's Friday, right? You have plans for later?"

"No, not me. Just a long day and too lazy to cook."

"I hear you," she said. "Story of my life. Every Friday I make a list of things to do on the weekend and on Monday I toss it having done none of them."

"I'll share a secret with you," I said, leaning forward. "Put it on the list when you do it, then cross it off. You'll always get at least one thing done."

She gave a polite laugh and moved down the counter to see to the other customers. I finished my salad and shoved the bowl aside, dabbing my mouth with the napkin.

"This seat taken?"

I looked over at John Kincaid, the Monarch detective, standing beside me.

"All yours," I said, sliding my salad bowl to the other side.

"Marlena, right? From the storage place?"

I nodded. "That's me. How are you, Detective?"

"John, please. I'm good. How about you? Any more excitement?" He slid onto the stool next to me.

"The storage business is probably the most boring job in the world."

"Oh, I don't know. You had some excitement last month. Anything new on that?"

"Not really," I began, then stopped and looked at him. "May I ask a question about the investigation?"

"Sure. Ask away. Although I can't divulge any top secret information," he said with a wink.

"Is it top secret?"

"Not that I know of," he said. "It's under wraps though. DEA and the drug task force don't want it broadcast. About the, uh, boxes you found. What can I help you with?"

"The two bodies that were found by the freeway. Is that your case?"

He nodded.

"Do you think they could be related?"

He thought for a minute. "You mean the boxes and the bodies?"

My turn to nod. "Yeah. Do you think they're related?"

He paused long enough to place his order before he answered me. "I don't see it myself. Why? Do you think they're related? Did you find something?"

I sipped tea and thought for a second. Burke was part of the task force, too. He told me he would turn in my information. I wondered if he did, or if he was just humoring me.

"Okay, this may be nothing," I said. "Did you get the file I sent, the one with the photo from our security camera? The guy walking around the back of the Move It truck?"

He shook his head and turned a little toward me. "First I've heard of it. When did you bring it in?"

"I didn't," I said. "I gave it to another guy in the group. He was going to turn it over to the task force. Maybe he forgot." Or maybe he tossed it, I thought. Maybe it never got reported.

"Who forgot? If you found something, anything, we need all the help we can get."

I took a deep breath. "I've been going over and over the videos from our cameras and I found a clip, just a quick shot really, of a guy coming around the back of a rental truck. I captured it and printed it out, along with the printed copy of who was in the lot at that time. Last night I saw the thing on the news, about those two men killed by the freeway."

John nodded and twirled a finger for me to go on.

"One of them, I think it was Esquibel, looked like the guy on my tape. I bought the paper last night to get the photos of them but no go. The paper didn't have them. Do you think I could get a copy of that segment from the news station?"

Kathy, the waitress, set down our meals. "I held yours up a little so you could eat together," she smiled. "Anything else I can get you?"

"I'll take some of that iced tea," John said. "How about you, Marlena?"

"I'm good, thanks."

John waited while Kathy brought his tea and wandered back up the counter. "I don't know the network's policy on copies," he said. "I don't know if they release them to the general public. You could ask."

I slumped a little and put down the piece of fish I was eating. Was it worth it? Was I just over reacting?

"Or," John continued, picking up a fry and dipping it in ketchup, "you could ask me and I could show you their pictures."

"You have them? Can I get copies?"

"Hang on a second," he said. "Let's reverse that. You give me what you have, the picture of the guy in your lot and I'll check them."

"I already gave the file to the task force," I said. "Evidently they didn't see the resemblance. I wanted another look at those men."

"I can double check with the DEA guys, or I can come by your office and take a look at what you have. I might even bring along my file. With the pictures of the expired gentlemen."

"Really?" I squealed, I know I did. "Can you bring them by my place? I don't work weekends and I don't want to wait till Monday. Sorry, I'm the impatient kind."

"Not a problem," he smiled. "What time tomorrow?"

"Whenever it's convenient," I smiled. "I really appreciate it. I'll be home all day."

"How about ten?"

"Perfect," I said, and leaned over to squeeze his hand. "Thank you."

"What the hell? Burke know you're cheating on him?" Even slurred I recognized the voice behind me.

Paul.

I looked over my shoulder to find him leaning on the stool next to me. The smell of alcohol made my eyes water. I pulled back.

He didn't notice, slid up on the stool and looked around me at Detective Kincaid. "Kincaid, right? Town cop?"

"Detective," John said. "And you're Paul Murphy. We've met."

"I thought that was you," Paul said, and tipped over. He had to slam a foot down and grab the counter to keep from losing his seat completely. "I'm not driving. Can't get me."

"Didn't plan on it," John said and picked up another fry. While polite you could have chilled beer with his voice. "Can I help you with something, Mr. Murphy?"

Paul lurched forward, almost toppling again, looking around me. "You can't. She could. She doing you, too? You know she's sleeping with Burke. You guys sharing her? She got a thing for cops?"

My face flamed and set my temper on fire. I slid off the stool and faced Paul. "I quit. You'll have it in writing tomorrow morning."

Paul tried to pat my arm and missed, patting thin air. "Now, don't get mad. I was just saying. You know I'd be interested myself if you get rid of the cops." His attempt at a smile was ludicrous, the saliva bubbling up at the corners of his mouth, his eyes at half-mast. He tilted sideways, clutching the counter to keep his seat. "You need to know there's options. I got more money than he does. Hell of a lot more than Burke." A string of drool dripped from his bottom lip to his shirt front.

Beside me John crumpled up his napkin, tossed it on the counter and stood up. He gently took my elbow and tugged me around to his side so he was facing Paul.

"How about we take a walk," he asked Paul, taking his arm. "I think you need some air."

"I think you better get your hands off me," Paul said with a slack grin. "Or you're gonna be looking for work. My dad's the mayor."

He tried to pull away from John and lost his balance again, this time sliding off his seat, his legs folding beneath him.

"You hit me again and I'm gonna sue," he slurred, clinging to the counter with both hands, trying to pull himself up.

"Sorry, Marlena," John said, edging me back a little further. "You'll have to excuse me and Mr. Murphy. Dinner is on me. I'll see you in the morning."

With that he pulled some bills from a front pocket and tossed them beside my plate. "After you, Mr. Murphy," he said to Paul, taking his arm and pulling him up and away from the counter. He turned him toward the door and gave him a little push.

Paul staggered and went down to his knees, throwing both hands out to break his fall.

"Got you now," he said, once he got his head upright. "That's police endangerment. Corruption or something."

"Brutality," John said, helping him up. "You're gonna learn about it up close and personal in about one minute. Now, let's take a little walk, shall we? Right across the street."

John had a firm grip on Paul's elbow and this time when he tugged Paul followed along although he was stumbling. John put his left arm around Paul's shoulders and used that to guide him out the front door. Paul made it as far as the curb before he suddenly doubled over and lost everything in the gutter.

Kathy, the waitress, shoved the folded bills toward me. "On the house tonight. Sorry about that. I hope you'll come back again soon."

I pushed the money back at her. "Not my money. Belongs to the detective."

She slipped it into her pocket. "I'll see he gets it back. I'm real sorry this happened. Can I get you some dessert? You can take it with you."

"No, thanks. Dinner was very good. I'm sorry, too."

"Not your fault," she said, shaking her head. "Usually he stays at the Gem when he gets like that."

"He does this a lot?"

Kathy's eyes got wide all of a sudden. "I wouldn't know," she said quickly. "Thank you again for your business. Hope to see you soon." With that she hurried down the counter, leaving me to wonder if my boss was also the town drunk.

I pulled out my keys and for the first time noticed everyone was looking at me. The whole place was silent, not even the clink of a fork. When I looked around everyone got busy looking the other way.

Well, terrific. I am now unemployed and the talk of the town.

I went home.

Chapter 10

I was through the first pot of coffee and started a second when John Kincaid knocked on the front door the next mornig. I let him in. He took a seat at the kitchen table while I poured him a cup of coffee. He had a manila folder in his hand.

"Just push those papers to the side," I said, bringing his coffee to the table.

He turned the sheets and glanced at them before shoving them aside. "What's this?"

"My official resignation," I said, picking up the papers and setting them on the counter. "I quit last night."

"I know. I was there. You really gonna leave?"

I brought my cup over and took a seat. "That's the idea."

John smiled. "I've taken Paul Murphy in a couple of times. He's gonna sleep till two and wake up in a brand new world. He won't remember a thing. Your job is safe, Marlena."

"I remember, John, and that's what matters. I only expect two things from a boss – respect and my paycheck on time. Paul can kiss my pearly pink fanny." I scooted over another folder. "This is the stuff I was talking about last night." I pulled out the photo I had copied from the DVD. "This guy here. I have checked and double checked. There is no record of him coming in. No code, no unit number, nothing. Not for that whole time period."

John took the picture and looked at it for a full minute before he pulled a photo from his own folder. He laid it beside the first and studied it. "I think you're right."

Yes! I wanted to dance. "You think they're the same?"

"I wouldn't put my life on it but yeah, I think they're the same. Can I keep this?" He lifted the picture I had printed.

"Sure. Take the whole file. There was supposed to be a copy given to the task force already. Thank you."

His brow wrinkled. "For what?"

"Believing me. Taking the time to at least look."

"Who did you show this to before?"

"Burke. The undercover guy. The one from the task force. He's been working here."

John nodded. "I'll check with him. The file may be at the office, overlooked. The bad thing about all these fingers in the pie is no one knows who the thumb is." He shook his head and smiled. "Don't get me wrong. These guys are good. All of them. They're just not used to working together. I'll be sure this gets brought to their attention. The DEA can send this to their lab, see what they can come up with. We could be wrong." He winked at me. "I don't think so."

"Thanks, John. I appreciate it. Even if it isn't him I thank you for at least listening to me."

"Hey, part of my job. Thank you for taking an interest. Now, can I ask you a personal question?"

"Ask away."

"Have you had trouble with Paul in the past?"

I sighed. "Not really. I haven't had that much to do with any of the family. Until the drug thing came along."

"I hope you know the law protects you from sexual harassment in the work place. I can get you some information if you'd like."

I laughed out loud. "I'm sorry," I said, still giggling. "I can handle myself, thank you. To be honest, I may have overreacted. Still, he made some ugly remarks last week, too. I didn't like it. So it may be time to move on before it gets worse."

"Can you tell me about it?"

"Oh, it wasn't physical, not anything like that." I sighed again. "Burke, the undercover guy. Do you know him?"

John nodded. "I've met him. I don't know him. I've never worked with him or anything. Is he a problem?"

"No, not at all. We've gotten to be friends, him being here so much. We have dinner, watch a movie, and sometimes go to dinner. Friends, you know?"

"Romantic? With either guy?"

"Oh, hell, no," I laughed. "Burke and I are friends. No benefits."

"You don't have to answer," John smiled. "I'm being kinda personal here."

"That's all right. We're just friends. He's been working a lot of hours. He fell asleep on the couch last week and I let him sleep. On the couch. The next morning I was in the shower, alone, when Paul came by. Burke answered the door, I was in the shower and he thought the worst."

"Still not his business," John said. "You weren't on the clock."

"No, it was early. I guess Paul and Burke have a history, goes back to high school. Some kind of rivalry. I didn't hear the conversation but I know Burke can be a smart ass. He may have hinted at something else, I don't know. Like I said, I didn't hear it."

"So Paul thought Burke spent the night. Not his business, rivalry or not. That's what he was going on about last night. Saying you were sleeping with him?"

I nodded again. "That's it. And then it was you. You made the mistake of sitting by me. I guess he thought you were sleeping with me, too."

"For the record, I consider that a compliment," he said. "I can talk to him if you'd like."

"No need. I'm done here. I won't have any more trouble with him."

Someone knocked on the front door and I jumped.

"Excuse me," I said, and went to the door.

Papa Murphy stood on the third step.

"Good morning," he said with a big smile.

"Good morning," I returned. "Come on in."

Papa Murphy came in the door then stopped short when he saw John at the table. He looked at me. "Is there a problem? Another one? Did something happen?"

"Not with the facility, Mr. Murphy. Everything here is fine. Have a seat. I'll get my resignation for you."

"What resignation? What's going on here?"

John stood and shook hands with the older gentleman. "John Kincaid, Mr. Murphy."

94

"I know who you are. I hired you. I want to know why you're here. What's going on?"

I picked up my resignation from the counter and handed it over. "Would you like a cup of coffee? Tea?"

Papa Smurf took the papers and sat down at the table. He glanced over the papers and put them to the side.

"I will have coffee," he said. "I only had one cup at Kelly's. I wanted to get here early, before you started your day."

I poured his coffee and took a seat. "What can I do for you, sir?"

"For a start you don't call me sir. Makes me feel old." He looked over at John. "Why are you here? Did she call the cops?"

John shook his head. "We had an appointment this morning."

Mr. Murphy looked between us then settled on John. "I don't understand. Why are you here?"

"You're aware we have an ongoing investigation here, sir. Regarding those drugs found in one of your units. We were doing an update."

"Nothing to do with us," Murphy snapped. "I personally talked to the District Attorney and we are completely clear."

"Never doubted you, sir," John said. "Miss Montoya had some information for us, regarding that case. I'm here to get that information. As a matter of fact, I was about ready to leave."

Murphy blinked. "This isn't about last night?"

"No sir. I took your son in last night on a separate note."

"You arrested him?"

"I detained him for his own good. He was drunk in public and disorderly. I took him in and let him sleep it off." John glanced at me. "Miss Montoya did not press charges, although she had the right to do so. Your son was abusive and insulting."

The senior Murphy met John's look before dropping his chin to look at his cup. The quiet spread like warm water. It was a full two minutes before Papa Smurf lifted his head, his eyes glistening. "My son has problems. I hope you will give my family the courtesy of keeping this among ourselves. We don't discuss it publicly. However, in this circumstance, I feel it's important." He cleared his throat and took a sip of coffee.

"My son has always dealt with disappointment. His goals even as a child were unreal, out of his reach and he kept trying. His first marriage was a complete disaster. They were too young, both of them. Still, he tried. He tried so hard." He shook his white head. "When that finally fell apart, he joined the Marines to get away from everything. He loved it. Loved it! Then he was excused, whatever that meant. We never understood. Oh, he has an honorable discharge, full benefits and all that. They just let him go. Sent him home. He was in Afghanistan at the time. Any way you don't care about that. The thing is he's been disappointed. In his choices. So he made another one, just as bad. Any set back now he turns to the bottle." He shook his head again. "Beer is not so bad. We try to limit even that. Still, there are times he turns to the bottle, the hard stuff. He'll only drink good Irish whiskey," he smiled. "He shouldn't drink at all. We try to watch him, keep him from embarrassing himself, the family."

"Sir, with all due respect to you and your family, Paul is a grown man. His behavior last night was out of line. You need to realize Marlena was within her rights to have him arrested."

"I know that, Detective Kincaid. Believe me, I know that very well. I'll deal with him. Right now I'm here to deal with you," he said and looked at me. He picked up my carefully written resignation and tore it in half, tossing the pieces back on the table. "There is no need for this. You are doing an excellent job. We're all pleased with your performance. As a matter of fact I'm here to tell you we've given you a raise. A sizeable one. We all agreed on that yesterday. Before last night's unfortunate incident. I hope you can overlook my son's behavior. That was inexcusable and I assure you I will speak to him about it." He got to his feet. "I'm going to assume this matter is closed and you will be in the office on Monday as usual."

"I appreciate your efforts, Mr. Murphy. I still think it would be best for all concerned if you found another manager."

"No," the old man said. "I refuse."

"Sir, Papa," I fumbled for the right words. "This is not going to work. I don't want to cause friction between you and your son, with your family. You have my notice. I'll stay till you find a new manager."

"Excellent. You stay till I find someone else, run the place as you have been." He stood up so I did. He reached out and caught my hand, holding it between both of his. "You've been excellent, turned this place around. I can't thank you enough for all you've done. Please, forgive Paul. I assure you it will not happen again. Let's put this whole thing behind us and forget it."

He shook hands with John and left quickly, closing the door behind him.

I stood at the door wondering what happened. I looked over at John. "Did I quit?"

John laughed. "I've dealt with that old man before. He's like a steam roller when he gets going. In answer to your question? No, I think he rejected your resignation."

"He said he'd find a new manager."

"Mm-hmm, he did. And he's not gonna find another manager in the next ten years. You stepped in that one, Marlena." He smiled and stood up to take his cup to the sink. "Can I say I'm happy about it? I was enjoying dinner last night before Paul showed up. I'd like to try it again. What do you say?"

"I'd like that. By the way, did you get your money back? The waitress, Kathy, tried to give it back to me."

"Haven't seen her yet. No big deal. I eat there a lot. Being single I don't cook much. If it won't go between two pieces of bread I don't buy it. Peanut butter is my best friend. I use the same coffee cup all week. Rinse it out daily and wash it on Sunday. Life of a bachelor. You're doing me a favor to have dinner with me."

"I look forward to it," I said. "Thank you for your help, with the Paul situation last night."

"Just doing my job, ma'am," he drawled. "How about tonight?"

"Sounds good," I smiled. "What time?"

"Six?"

"I'll be ready."

"All right, I'll see you then." With another smile he picked up the folders, both his and mine, and let himself out, closing the door behind him.

I got yet another cup of coffee and sat back down at the table. The two halves of my resignation letter laid where they had fallen. I wadded them up and tossed them at the trash can.

I liked my job, I liked Mr. and Mrs. Murphy and I had no problem with Patrick. If Paul stayed out of my way this could work. If not? I had saved the letter on my computer. I could reprint it in minutes.

My afternoon nap was interrupted by the delivery of flowers, a sweet smelling selection of lilies and carnations. No card. I was pretty sure a Murphy was behind the gesture. I just didn't know which one.

~~~

My weekend was relaxing and I needed it after the strain of the past few weeks. Late nights reading reams of logs, long hours watching the recorded videos and the incident with Paul Murphy all backed up on me and I was happy to take a break from all of it.

John and I drove all the way down to San Luis Obispo for dinner on Saturday night. Restaurant choices in this area are slim if you want something besides bar food or Kelly's Diner. There was also no chance of running into a Murphy.

Sunday I drove up to Singer Lake with a picnic lunch and my Kindle. Sometimes it's nice to be away from everything and everyone. I returned home relaxed and ready for the week.

That was asking for it.

Chapter 11

Monday morning I made the coffee in the office and sipped a cup while watching the weekend's tapes from the cameras. Nothing out of the ordinary. The phantom Burke made no appearances I could see, everything normal.

Two hours later John walked in.

"Good morning," I said. "What can I do for you this fine morning?"

"You're in a good mood," he smiled. "Most folks are grumpy on Monday."

"I'm not most folks," I smiled back.

"I'll go along with that. I sure enjoyed dinner Saturday night. I hope we can do it again real soon."

"Any time. I had a good time, too."

He double patted the counter and glanced around the office. "I'd rather talk about Saturday but I'm here on business. Do you have another copy of that file you turned in? I dropped it off at the Sheriff's department, for the task force and they've lost it. Can't find it anywhere. I thought you might give me another copy."

"Sure. I keep copies of everything. Covers my fanny," I said. "Let me get it and I'll run you another copy." I stepped into the back office to get the file from the cabinet.

It wasn't there. I double checked, going back through the last three months in case I had misfiled it. No luck. I looked all over my desk, checked the shelf where the manila folders are kept, everywhere. Nothing. I went back to the front office.

"Hang on a minute. I guess I misplaced it," I said, looking through the desk drawers, although I was sure I had filed it in back. Another five minutes produced nothing.

"I am so sorry. I can't find it. I had it a few days ago, when I gave the copies to you and now I can't find it anywhere. Can you hang on a few more minutes while I run upstairs and check?"

"Sure, Marlena, take your time. I'll get some of that coffee if it's okay."

"In the back room," I pointed to the break room door. "Help yourself, cream in the fridge. I'll be right back."

I went out the back door and hurried up the stairs, trying to remember the last time I saw the file folder. I was sure I had filed it after showing it to John. I remembered sliding it in the file cabinet because I had to make a new folder for it, not wanting it confused with the normal back up files I keep for the business.

Nothing. I checked the living room, kitchen, even my bedroom and there was no manila folder.

I didn't lose it. Someone took it. I'm not perfect but I am also not one of those who loses their car keys or misplaces their checkbook. I pride myself on my memory.

The folder was gone.

I hurried back downstairs, again using the back door, and went into the office to find Patrick Murphy talking to John.

While I had never formally met Patrick, I had seen him on the cameras often, helping his mom load or unload. Up close he was a lot bigger than the little figure I had watched. As tall and broad as John with that deep black hair that shines almost blue in the sun and piercing bright blue eyes. His face was shadowed by a mustache and beard, both as black as his hair, making those eyes stand out.

"Oh, I'm sorry, I didn't know you were here," I said, extending my hand to shake with him. "I'm Marlena Montoya. We haven't met. Can I help you?"

The look he gave me would have frozen water. He ignored my outstretched hand and leaned on the counter.

"I know who you are," he said. "I sign your paychecks." His voice was as cold and hard as concrete in winter. "I don't pay this guy, I pay you. Where were you?"

Deep breath, I thought, and blew it out. "This is Detective John Kincaid from Monarch," I said, indicating John with one hand. "He's working with the drug task force."

Patrick Murphy flipped a hand. "I know who he is. He's not on the payroll. Where were you? Aren't you supposed to be working?"

Okay, one more deep breath. "I was upstairs looking for a file for Detective Kincaid, one I seem to have misplaced. I was not gone more than five minutes."

"So where's this file?"

"I just told you, I seem to have misplaced it. I'm sorry you had to wait. Is there something I can do for you?"

"Yeah, there is. I keep my motor home in space 29. I have for years. Now it's occupied by another motor home. I believe your job includes seeing that everyone is where they belong. I want it moved. Do your job and get it out of my way. *Comprende?*"

"Yes, I understand. I was not aware you used that space. There is no record of it while I've been here. I will have the gentleman move. Is there anything else?"

Patrick gave me another of his frozen looks, turned and left without another word. I heard his truck start and looked out the window to see him drive away.

"Nice guy," John said.

"Sorry about that," I said, yet another apology.

"Hey, no problem. Looks like a genetic defect. Probably the first in his family born without a tail."

I chuckled. "Well, I've never met him before. Not personally, although I know the whole family. He seems to have missed the courtesy gene." I spread my hands, palms up. "I am really sorry but that file is gone. I can't find it."

"Can you make another one?"

I thought back. "Yes, I can. It will take me a little bit, to get the data off the recorder. Once I find the date I can burn the DVD in minutes. Can you wait?"

"I can do that."

"Let me find my copy," I said. I went to the back office and to get last month's DVD. At the end of every month I burn the camera recordings to a DVD and file it on a shelf with the others. Each one goes into a glassine envelope with the date on the front so they're easy to find.

Last month was missing.

I checked, rechecked and looked again. Two were missing. Last month and the month before. I was sure I had only used the one from the previous month.

"I'm sorry," I told John, on my way through the office. "I must have left it upstairs. I'll be right back."

Once more up the stairs I hurried through the apartment checking my desk, the table and the counters, the only places I ever lay down work related documents. The DVD's were missing.

Back downstairs I looked at John and shrugged. "No idea. Something is weird," I said. "I am not careless with company records. They're missing. The last two months are gone and I have no idea where."

"Who else has access to this office," John asked. "Could someone have taken them?"

"I suppose, but why? As for keys I have my keys. Steve, the weekend guy, has a set for the front door and the overlocks. Burke doesn't have keys. He comes in when the office is open."

"Burke?"

"Detective Burke. Agent Burke. Whatever he is, he's on the task force. He's the undercover guy here. Declan Burke."

"Oh, right. I forgot. So the only door keys are yours and this Steve's?"

I thought about it. "The owners have keys. They must have."

John pulled a small spiral notebook from his shirt pocket. "The Murphy's," he said. "All of them?" He took a pen from the cup on the counter and turned to a new page.

"I don't know," I said. "I've never asked. I'm assuming at least one of them has keys. They own the place. What if I took off? Was in a wreck or something. There must be another set. At least one."

John put the pen back. "There could be more?"

I nodded. "I've only been here a couple of years. Who knows? The previous managers could still have keys. I never asked if they changed the locks. Could even be a former employee if they didn't change them out."

John frowned and put the notebook back in his pocket. "So a lot of people have access to this office."

Put like that it sounded sloppy, like anyone could wander in when no one was around. "I hate to say it, but yeah, I guess so."

"How about customers? Could they go back there?"

"They could I guess but I don't leave them here alone. If I'm showing a unit or cleaning on the lot or whatever, I lock the doors." I held up the small plastic sign with the Velcro back that read 'Manager Outside, Please Wait' in tall, black letters. "This goes on the front door and I lock it. Even when I go get the mail."

"You left me here, unattended," he reminded me.

I felt my cheeks flush. "You don't count." I rolled my eyes and sighed. "That didn't come out right. You know what I mean. You're a cop."

"I got it," he smiled. "Is there anyone else you leave here?"

"I don't think so."

"How about Burke?"

"Possible," I said. "He uses the back door, to get to the tools and the cart. I may have left it unlocked during the day. It's an unmarked door and most customers don't even know it's there. It opens into the garage."

"Burke could come in through the garage, to here, in the office. Is that right?"

I nodded again. "He could. But he's a cop, too."

"How about when you close? Can the garage be opened? From the outside?"

"No. There's an automatic door opener we use to open it. From the inside there's a button to lift the door but not from the outside."

"Okay. Then if you were outside without an opener how would you get in the garage?"

"Come through here, either the back or the front, go into the garage and push the door lift from inside."

"Well, that's no help," he smiled. "I'll go search the Sheriff's department. There's one room up there the task force is using as a base of operations. Someone may have misplaced it, or borrowed it and forgot to bring it back. I'll check with them. In the meantime, do you think you could ask about the keys?"

"I intend to. Truthfully, I doubt they know. I've found Mrs. Murphy's keys half a dozen times. She lays them on the ground, or the roof of her car and drives off and the keys fall off."

"They're separate from her car keys? She could leave them and not know it?"

"And does. Half a dozen times at least. I've found them."

"They could leave them around the house, too. Even around the Gem."

I nodded. The security blanket was moth eaten at best.

John thought for a few minutes, his brow furrowing. "Do you have the authority to change the locks? The ones to the front and back doors?"

"I suppose. We have an open account at the hardware store in Monarch. I charge whatever I need for repairs around here. I turn in the charge slips with the end of month reports."

"You might want to do that," John said. "Personally? I think you should at least change the locks on the apartment. With that many keys floating around, better safe than sorry."

"I'll do that," I said. "Tonight. I don't think I'd sleep well now."

"Tell you what," John said, "how about I pick up the lock and a pizza and bring it over after work."

"If you let me pay for the lock, you have a deal."

"Fair enough," he smiled. "In the meantime I'm going to check with the rest of the team, see if anyone remembers that file, maybe moved it or borrowed it. I'll see you tonight. Office closes at five?"

"Yes it does. And I need time for a shower."

"We'll make it six then. That work?"

"Perfect," I said with my own smile.

John doubled patted the counter again and left.

I went to the back office for one more look around. The idea of someone being in here bothered me. Deposits I took upstairs with me. We kept a hundred dollars on hand in the office to make change or use for petty cash. Hardly worth a break in. The most expensive items in the office were the software programs and those were useless to almost everyone.

108

I decided to ask Papa Murphy about changing the locks rather than do it without authorization although I couldn't see a reason they would object. After all, it was their property. I'd think they would want it secure. As for the customers, they had keys for their own locks, unless they were overlocked and the overlock key was a master key.

I could see why the Murphy men had keys to the office. They had trouble with managers in the past. They explained that when they hired me. Various times one or the other had to run the office. They needed keys. Mrs. Murphy never worked in the office. Her keys should be the ones for the units she occupied.

Changing the locks would require four duplicates – one for each of the Murphy men and one for Steve on weekends. Four extra keys. Was it worth it? That would have to be up to Papa Murphy. As for my apartment? Papa would need a key, he owned the place. The others? Nada. If they needed in my apartment they could make an appointment.

Now I was faced with the fact that someone had taken those DVD's from the back office, my office, the one off limits to Steve. They weren't hidden, they were kept in a cabinet in the back along with the video recorder. Who was in here? I made a note to ask Steve on Saturday if any of the owners had been in on the weekend.

There was nothing I could do now, this afternoon, so I went back to work.

At five I went through the closing routine and backed up all the video on the cameras. The office closes at five, with paid customers allowed access until seven. While the computers did their jobs, I used the camera system to take a last look around the lot.

In checking the property I noticed Burke's motor home in space 29. Which reminded me of Patrick's complaint. I had left a message on Burke's cell phone. He never responded.

I tried again and again it went to voice mail. I left another request to move it.

On a whim I wrote up a quick note, got the cart and drove out to tape the note to the door of the motor home. If something had happened to Burke's phone, he surely would see this the next time he was here.

John was punctual and even better, he was a football fan. Fortunately, neither of us had a favorite playing on Monday Night Football so we spent an enjoyable evening.

After the game John changed the lock on the front door and presented me with a pair of keys when he was finished. Neither of us mentioned the missing files.

Chapter 12

Tuesday morning I opened the office as usual.

No messages from Burke.

I still had to get that motor home moved. I left another message on his voice mail, got the cart and went out to check his motor home.

My note was still attached to the door. The tape looked undisturbed.

Heading back to the office I saw Patrick's truck. I only met him recently but I had spent a lot of hours watching him pack, repack and unload his mother's units. Several times I had observed him laughing with her. Once he picked her up and swung her around in a circle while she squealed, her hands on his broad shoulders.

My memories of the guy I observed on camera were a whole lot warmer than the cold, abrupt man I met last night.

I changed direction and headed for his truck, wondering which Patrick was present today.

I pulled the cart up close to the door and hailed him. He materialized from the gloom inside the storage unit like a ghost and drifted to the door.

"I wanted to let you know I didn't forget about your motor home. I've left messages for the owner to move his. He appears to be out of town. I'll keep after him."

"Why is he there?"

"I'm sorry about that. My records show that space empty. I wasn't aware you used it."

"I've always used it," he replied.

"You haven't used it since I've been here," I said, annoyed at this attitude. "My customer list says the space is vacant."

"I'm not a customer," he snapped back. "I'm the owner. I own that space and I want it."

"I understand that, Mr. Murphy, and I am doing all I can do to get it ready for you."

"Patrick. My dad is Mr. Murphy."

"Well, Patrick, I am still doing all I can do to get that motor home moved. I will mark the space as occupied as soon as I do."

"Who owns that motor home? Maybe I know him."

"I doubt you'd know him," I said and was interrupted.

"How long have you lived here?"

"Almost two years," I answered and again was stopped from saying more.

"I've been here thirty. This is one of several businesses we own. I'd be willing to bet I know more people here than you do."

"Yes, sir, I'm sure you do. We've had an incident here," and again I was cut off.

"I know about the drugs. So is this guy a suspect? Is the law watching him or something?"

I took in a deep breath and let it out slowly. "He is the law. He's with the CCID. He's watching the property."

"Is he paying for that space?"

"No, sir."

"Then he moves. Out if necessary. We run this business for profit. If he's staying he's paying."

My temper was on the rise and I was fighting to keep it in check. I couldn't afford to cross another boss if I wanted to keep my job. The big question was did I want to keep my job?

"Yes, sir," I said between gritted teeth. "I'll see to it."

"And I'm not 'sir'."

"Of course, Patrick," I said, managing to make the name sound venomous.

He stood for a minute looking me up and down with those cold eyes before turning his back and disappearing back into the unit. The interior darkness swallowed him.

I started the cart and drove back to the office, sure the camera would show smoke coming out of my ears. If Burke didn't answer my calls by tonight I was going to have the motor home towed and the cost of that would come from my own pocket. The last time I was going to have a run in with a boss.

Too many bosses.

While I liked and admired Papa Murphy he had failed to teach his sons courtesy. First the Paul incident, then this.

I was going to print out my resume.

Tonight.

I left yet another message on Burke's voice mail, then rooted around for Agent Miller's card. I dialed that number and got another machine. Technology.

I wondered if the task force played golf all day and checked their messages once a week.

~~~

The next day I looked up the number for a towing company and made an appointment for the afternoon which set my mood for the day.

Still no Burke.

He had gone from being a semi-permanent fixture to a pale memory in just a few weeks. What's with this guy? From easy companion and outrageous flirt to missing in action.

With that thought came the hope he was all right. I had no idea what Burke did when he wasn't here. Several times he had been absent for a few days, never this long. A sniggle of guilt nested in the back of my mind, right beside the memory of the two dead men found alongside the freeway.

I sent up a silent prayer Burke wasn't going to be found the same way.

The tow truck came and moved the motor home and fifty bucks transferred from my checking account to his.

The new space was only two slots over so Burke could find it if he showed up. I didn't bother to notify Patrick his space was clear but I did take that space off the rentals list so I didn't make the same mistake again.

The rest of the day was routine. I was happy to see it. After the drama of the past few days it was nice to sit in the office and crunch numbers. Randy came in and spent an hour updating me on the state of the nation.

Things slowly slid down the slope into normal.

Friday I was looking forward to the weekend. It was a tossup between locking the door and watching old movies or running away to Cambria for a couple of days.

For almost two years my day and my social interaction ended at five o'clock. The past weeks with Burke, and then John, coming by had filled my evenings.

I reluctantly admitted to myself that I missed them, or more accurately, I missed the company.

When I locked up the office, I headed to Kelly's in Monarch. Rather a diner full of strangers than an empty living room.

Being early on a Friday night I had my pick of places to sit so I took a booth. Kathy, the waitress I knew slightly, came right over to take my order.

"Hey, good to see you," she said, pulling out her order pad. "You're getting to be a regular here. What can I get you this evening?"

"I'll have the special and iced tea."

"Coming right up."

She went back up front to place my order. I opened my Kindle.

The diner wasn't full although there were enough people to make a low hum of conversation just audible over the clink of silverware. A comfortable level of white noise.

I read a few pages before Kathy brought my tea.

"Here you go," she smiled, putting down a coaster and a straw. "I'm happy to see you. After the last time, I was afraid you wouldn't be back."

"Wasn't your fault," I said, closing the Kindle.

"No, it wasn't. You know how it is. Someone has a bad experience they don't want to go back, you know? Avoid the scene of the crime."

"I wouldn't hold it against Kelly's," I said with a smile of my own. "Can't be responsible for the way others behave. Not likely to run into that guy again."

Kathy's eyes rounded and she took on an owl look. "What? Is he here?"

The waitress nodded and tipped her head towards the front of the diner. "He's near the door up there. He's sober, though, so you're okay. It's only when he's drinking that he gets, well, rowdy? The rest of the time he's a doll, he really is."

"Does he drink a lot?"

"I wouldn't know," she backtracked. "He's come in happy a few times. You know? When he's had a good day and he wants to share it? He helps his dad at the Gem so sometimes he's had a few?"

Her habit of adding a question mark at the end of a sentence made it difficult to know if she was telling me or asking me. I opted for a nod and sipped tea.

"I'll get your fish," she said and left the table, back in a minute with my order.

I picked up my Kindle again.

"It's rude to read at the table," a voice said and I looked up to see Patrick Murphy slide into the booth across from me.

I closed the Kindle. Now what?

"Your space is clear," I said, as politely as possible. "You can bring your motor home down any time. That won't happen again."

"All business, huh? I saw the tow truck," he said. "I was working in my mom's unit when he came in."

"I'm very sorry that happened," I said, tired of apologizing.

"What are you reading?" He turned to signal Kathy, who hurried back to our table.

"Along Came a Spider," I said.

"James Patterson," he said to me. "Can I get some coffee, Kat?"

The waitress nodded and hurried away.

"Yes, it is," I said, surprised Patrick would know that.

"Good book. I liked it."

"You read?"

He nodded and smiled at me. "I'm not ignorant, Miss Montoya. Nor am I stupid. I read a lot."

"I meant no offense," I said, feeling my cheeks warm up. "Most guys like you don't read," I stopped in mid-sentence. His eyes were laughing. "There's no way I'm going to get out of that one," I said.

To my surprise he laughed. He had a contagious laugh. I found myself joining in.

I started again. "I meant guys who look like you don't usually read."

"What's wrong with the way I look?"

"Not a thing," I blurted, before I blushed to my hairline, feeling the heat in my face. "I am so sorry. That didn't come out right."

Patrick Murphy smiled a slow, warm smile, his blue eyes lighting up. "Go ahead," he said. "It's fun to watch you blush. Don't see that much anymore."

I ducked my head and sipped tea, listening to his chuckle. "Let me start over," I said. "So you liked the book?"

Patrick leaned forward on his folded arms. "I did. It was similar to a Michael Crichton, another favorite of mine. I have also read most of the classics. I like Rex Stout, Robert Parker and I read the Tarzan series twice when I was a kid."

"You like mysteries and adventure," I smiled.

"I like books," he said and sat back for Kathy to set a cup of coffee down in front of him. I had never seen that kind of service.

Kelly's kept a tray of clean mismatched cups next to the front door. If you wanted coffee you chose a cup when you came in and carried it to your seat. Tourists and visitors were marked when they made the return trip to pick up a cup.

This was a first, seeing a wait person bring a cup. Patrick must rate around here.

"Would you like anything else?"

"Not right now, thanks."

The waitress scurried back to the front. If she had a forelock she'd have yanked it out by the roots.

Patrick returned his attention to me. "How do you like that Kindle?"

"I love it," I answered, happy to change the subject. "I read a lot, too. With this I don't have to drive to a book store, or wait for one to open. I can browse books in the middle of the night and sample them before I pay. They offer samples for free. If it doesn't sound interesting, I can delete it and move one to the next one. Sort of like browsing in a book store. Of course I'm limited to Amazon but that's my favorite place to shop anyway, so for me its fine."

"I've thought about getting one but I like the feel of a book, the weight, you know?"

"I do," I agreed. "I wasn't sure I'd like one until about ten minutes after I bought it. Took that long for me to fall in love."

"You do that a lot?"

"Excuse me?"

"Fall in love. You do that a lot?"

Before I could answer Kathy came back and looked at my plate. "Are you finished with that?"

There were still a couple of pieces of fish and some fries on the plate.

"Yes, thanks," I said, although I wanted the fish I didn't want to eat in front of Patrick. I slid the plate closer to her.

"More tea? Some dessert? We have apple, berry and peach fruit pies and banana and coconut cream. From Cora's bakery right here in town."

"I'll have the apple," Patrick said. "How about you?"

"I'm good," I said.

"Come on," he smiled. "Pick one or I'll pick it for you."

I thought for a second. "Peach," I said.

"Ice cream?"

"No, the pie is fine."

Kathy left again, leaving me and Patrick looking at each other.

"You want to talk more books? Move on to movies? History? Foreign languages? I am well versed I assure you." He was smiling at me.

I felt the heat climbing up my neck again, the flush like a sunburn. "I'm kinda boring," I said finally. "I read a lot, I like the old movies on TV."

"Me too. What are your favorites?"

"Most of the black and white ones from the forties and fifties. The mysteries. I love the funny ones, the ones where everyone gets stuck in an old house and picked off one at a time."

His eyes glowed bright blue. "Where the eyes in the picture on the wall move? And there's about eight bedrooms with secret passages and one creepy butler?"

My turn to nod. "That's them. And the Thin Man, Charlie Chan, all those."

"Topper? I loved the Topper movies. I collected them. Topper and W.C. Fields."

"I love those! Charlie McCarthy and Mortimer Snerd. I remember them and the westerns. So many westerns."

"No brothers or sisters?"

"Two of each. I was the youngest. We had one of those aerials on top of the house. No cable or dish so it was old movies or nothing. I got parked in front of the TV while they all worked."

I stopped when Kathy slid our desserts onto the table. She didn't even glance my way, focused on Patrick. "More coffee?"

"Yeah, thanks. How about you? Would you like coffee?"

I nodded, my mouth full of luscious golden peaches.

"She'll have coffee, too," he told the waitress who once more hurried away only to return with another cup and the pot of coffee. A double first – two cups brought to the table. I'd have to remember that my next trip, see if it was a new policy.

"Will there be anything else?"

"Should do us," Patrick said, forking up a chunk of apple pie. "I'll wave if we need anything else."

Kathy left again, with a wistful look over her shoulder that was wasted on Patrick. He was watching me.

We continued to chat about old movies while we ate our desserts.

Kathy brought our checks and Patrick picked up both slips.

"I can get mine," I said. "After all you didn't have dinner."

Patrick smiled and handed over the checks and his credit card. "My pleasure," he said. "It's been a while since I had the company of a lovely woman."

Again the heat flashed up my neck into my face like filling a glass, even the tips of my ears were burning.

To my complete embarrassment Patrick burst out laughing. He laughed for a couple of minutes before taking a napkin and wiping his eyes.

"I'm glad you find me so amusing," I said.

He reached across the table and took my hand, giving my fingers a squeeze. "I apologize," he said, still grinning. "It's just fun to watch you blush. Like a thermometer the way it climbs up your neck. I couldn't resist."

I tossed my napkin on the table and gathered my keys and Kindle.

"Thanks for dinner," I said, scooting to the edge of the bench seat.

121

He held on to my hand. "Don't go away mad," he said. "I said I was sorry."

"I'm not mad. I'm tired. It's been a long day."

He looked at me for a full minute, holding me there by the hand. "What's on the agenda for tomorrow? You working?"

"I don't work weekends," I answered. "A very nice man named Steve runs the facility on weekends."

He nodded and released my hand. "I know. I sign his paycheck, too. He talks too much."

My turn to smile. "Yes, he does. He's reliable though. He's never late and he's always there."

"Probably looking for a captive audience," he smiled back.

I stood up. "Thank you for dinner. That was very nice of you."

"I'm a nice man," he answered with those dancing blue eyes. "Don't believe all you hear."

"I never do," I said and headed for the front door. Behind me a warm chuckle followed me to the door.

On the short drive back to Jade Beach my mind chased its tail.

I'm tall for a Latina, most of our women are shorter. I have black hair and brown eyes, the lighter caramel colored eyes not the deep mysterious brown ones. I stay in shape without effort, being on the slender side, a gift from my Indonesian mother, along with the almond shaped eyes tipped up at the corners and the paler, ivory skin. Without vanity I know I look good for my age, which is closing in on forty.

My years here that went unnoticed. Now, all of a sudden, I find not one, not two, but four handsome men want to share my meals. I wondered why. I don't put a whole lot of eggs in the coincidence basket.

Meeting Burke was bizarre. The whole beach scene and the guys chasing him into my car was weird. Then he showed up at my door.

The cartons of drugs brought Burke back into the picture. Also added John Kincaid as the local liaison so two connected to the drugs.

I had dealt with Paul since I took this job. Why his sudden interest? Was it finding Burke in my apartment first thing in the morning? Did that somehow trigger their old rivalry?

Patrick the playboy, the perpetual bachelor, hunted like prey by the single women in town. What caused him to come at me out of the blue? He never bothered to introduce himself until recently, our few meetings were official and cool. Why did he join me for dinner?

And where was Burke? Had something happened to him? Had his undercover persona been exposed? Two men had been murdered and dumped near the freeway, the first murders here in many years. Was that connected to the drugs? Was Burke dumped somewhere with a bullet in his head?

My mind whirled like a roulette wheel. Round and round and round we go, where we stop nobody knows. I began to feel like Alice in Wonderland – curiouser and curiouser.

It was a long time before I fell asleep.

Chapter 13

Saturday morning I drove to San Luis Obispo and spent the day wandering around the narrow, tree shaded streets doing a little shopping and catching a movie. I returned tired and rested if that makes any sense.

Sunday I hung around the house and did the chores I neglected yesterday.

Monday morning was heavy with fog, the thick wet kind that chilled to the bone. From the harbor the mournful fog horns sounded like lovesick cows and added to the atmosphere.

After I opened the office I made coffee, poured a cup and went up front, my plans to work outside shelved until the weather cleared.

Only one thing to do on a day like this – I turned on the heater and picked up my Kindle. I read one chapter before the front door opened and a Seattle Seahawks cap sailed in to land on the counter.

Burke was right behind it.

"Welcome back," I said, putting aside the Kindle.

"Got back last night. It was late so I didn't bother you. Who moved my motor home?"

"I had it moved," I said. "When you didn't return the dozen or so messages I left on your cell I called a tow truck. They moved it."

"Ah, then the next question is easy. Why?"

"That space was already rented."

"They couldn't take another one? It had to be that one?"

"Owner's prerogative."

Burke blinked. "Owner? Paul?"

"Patrick," I said, with a quick memory of bright blue eyes.

"Trick has a motor home? Hmm. Traveling bedroom I guess," he said with a grin. "Gotta watch that guy every minute."

"You know him, too?"

"Oh, yeah. Paul's little brother. He always called him Little Bother when we were kids. Papa Murphy always wanted the boys to be close." Burke shook his head at some memory. "That didn't work," he said.

"The boys aren't close?"

"Hardly," Burke snorted.

"How come?"

"Why the sudden interest?"

"I work for them," I said. "Can't hurt to know all I can."

Burke took a seat, leaned back in his chair and folded his arms. "Well, let's see. Paul was the golden child. Best of the best of the best. Did everything – academics, sports, you name it. When the paper came out on Friday there was always a Paul story somewhere."

"Patrick couldn't compete?"

"Patrick didn't try. Quiet kid, stayed out of the way. Paul picked on him a lot until Trick got some size on him. Paul went into the Marines, then to college, married into money, all the things Papa Murphy wanted." Burke chuckled. "A regular Irish American Prince."

"And?"

"That's it. Trick graduated from high school and took off. He was gone for a long time, no one knew where. Showed back up a couple of years ago. Papa put him back in the business and there you have it. Prodigal son kind of thing. Since then he's been working his way through all the women in the county. Can I get a cup of that coffee?"

"You know where it is," I said and watched him head for the kitchen. He was back in minutes and set his cup on the counter, walking around and pulling me up from my chair.

"I've missed you," he said, kissing me, pulling me closer.

I pushed him back and sat down. "Drink your coffee before it gets cold."

He looked a little put out but did as I asked and sat down. On the other side of the counter. "Not much of a welcome there. Didn't you miss me at all?" He sounded like a petulant teenager.

"Were you gone?"

He chuckled again. "Uh – huh. You left me enough messages."

"About the motor home," I said. "Nothing personal."

"Well, I did notice you didn't leave any undying love declarations although I was hoping."

I looked at him. No need to answer that one. "Working on the case?"

He nodded and sighed. "I should have told you I was going out of town. Is that what you're ticked off about?"

"Not ticked off, Burke."

"Whoa, a little testy there, Marlie."

"Marlie?"

He chuckled again. "Marlena is a mouthful, babe. I'll just call you Marlie."

"Most people call me Marlie."

"Good. I like it better."

I shook my head at him. "What else have you been up to, Burke? You said you got back. From where?"

"See? I knew you missed me. How about dinner tonight and I'll fill you in. Pizza? Or you want to cook me a welcome home dinner?"

"How about neither. Not tonight, sorry."

"You have other plans?"

I nodded at him, not wanting to lie. "Maybe next time."

"Okay, then," he said, standing. "I see I've been excused. Guess I'll get to work. How about tomorrow night? You booked for that, too?"

"No," I said.

"Then dinner tomorrow night is on me. And I'll bring you up to date on where I've been. I have to check in with the task force, talk to the guys and see if they've turned up anything new."

"I'm sure they'll give you an update," I said. "I'm not part of the group."

Burke furrowed his brow and looked at me. "You okay? You sound kinda miffed. I couldn't return your calls, Marlena. I don't carry my cell. That could be trouble in the wrong hands."

"No need to explain, Burke. You're not responsible to me. For anything. I'm not your boss."

"You're more," he said, his dark eyes glowing. "And you know it."

Before I could think of a response he was gone, out the front door. I heard his truck start and then fade away.

The entry and exit controls for the facility gates are mounted on heavy poles on the left side so drivers don't have to exit their vehicles to put in their code.

Rarely used, unless it's raining, is an intercom system, also mounted inside the key pad box. A customer can push the button and speak to the office without having to get out of his or her vehicle.

The other side of that particular coin is that the microphone is always open. I can hear anything said in the vehicle while the customer is next to the controls. Few know it and even those ignore it.

I find it amusing to hear the names I get called when they're locked out.

Accidental eavesdropping goes with the job.

After Burke left Paul pulled up at the gate, his cell phone pressed to his ear. He was arguing with someone. In Spanish.

I don't speak much Spanish which is surprising since my father is Mexican. My dad was proud of his American citizenship, always reminding us how lucky we were to be born here. When we were growing up he insisted on speaking English in the home because, he explained, we were Americans.

128

With my looks and my name a lot of people over the years spoke to me in Spanish and received a blank look. I picked up a few of the common phrases like everyone else in California but I was nowhere close to fluent. The best I could do was order in a Mexican restaurant, although I could roll my 'r's' with the best of them.

I didn't understand what Paul was saying but I did know he wasn't ordering food. Now, that's an odd thing for a family so proud of its Irish heritage. I doubted Papa Murphy spoke a lot of Spanish around the house. Perhaps Paul picked it up from his customers. I shrugged it off and went on with my day.

Having told Burke I had plans for dinner I headed over to Kelly's after the office closed. The Monday special is always the same – pot roast. It comes with carrots and potatoes and is soaked with rich, brown gravy. One of my favorites. Being single I rarely bothered to cook big meals. If I cooked a pot roast the leftovers would last a week.

The smell of the fog was heavy in Monarch, announcing its presence in advance. I could see it laying offshore, a thick gray curtain blending into the sea, giving the unsettling illusion of driving below sea level.

Inside I bypassed the trays of cups at the front door and took a seat at the counter, near the back. There were a couple of empty booths but I left those for larger parties.

Kathy came to take my order and when I asked for coffee she pointed up front. "You know where the cups are," she said with a smile softening her words. "I'll put in your order." With that she went up front.

I gathered a Murphy surname was necessary to have your cup delivered to your table, a theory I wanted to test one day.

With a sigh I got up and went to retrieve a cup. When I returned the stool beside me was occupied.

By John Kincaid.

"Thought that was you," he said when I regained my seat. "You meeting someone?"

"Just the waitress," I smiled.

"Great, let's get a booth," he said, and led the way to an empty one. With one hand on my back he guided me in before sliding into the seat across from me. "This is much better," he said when we were settled. "Have you ordered?"

"Yep," I nodded. "I got the special."

"Sounds good," he said. "I'm gonna go add mine. Be right back. You want anything to drink?"

I held up my cup and he left me to go place his order.

He was back in minutes with his own cup. "Few more minutes," he said. "I asked. So what's going on with you?"

"Nothing new," I said. "Same old thing, different day."

"You find those disks?"

"No, and I double checked again. Upstairs and downstairs. They're gone."

John sat back and sighed. "I didn't think you'd find them. I think someone took them. That 'someone' is a person of interest. I'd sure like to talk to him. Or her."

"Her? I can't think of a single woman that's been in the back office."

"How about a married one?"

I looked at him and he grinned. "Couldn't resist. It's the people I hang out with. Gets to be a habit. Sorry."

"No need. That was pretty quick. I'll have to practice."

He ran a hand through his hair. "Been a long day. I'm glad I ran into you, I wanted to talk to you."

"What about?"

We were interrupted by Kathy setting our dinners on the table.

"Now what was it you wanted to know," I asked when she went back up front.

"To begin with, the DEA ran that partial photo through some lab they have and according to Agent Miller they have a 75 per cent identification of Esquibel. Considering the angle and all the scientific stuff that I have no clue how works they think it's him. We are proceeding on that assumption."

"The guy on my tape, in my facility, is one of the men murdered and dumped near the freeway."

"Yes ma'am."

"Which connects him to the drugs."

"Yes ma'am."

"Do you think you might call me Marlie? My mother is ma'am."

"Yes, Marlie," he grinned.

I ate a couple of bites and took a sip of coffee. The dead men were now connected to my facility. The drugs were found in my facility. I'm smart enough to tie those two together. My immediate problem was being smart enough to figure whoever took the disks was also involved. Someone tied to the drugs was in my office.

The office just below where I lived. I drank more coffee.

"I see you got it," John said with a warm smile.

"Got what?"

"The connections. I can see the wheels turning in that pretty head of yours."

I hoped he couldn't see the other connections I made at the same time. Four men. All popped into my life right about the same time as the drugs. And I was convinced one of them was involved. At least one.

"Share," John said, drawing me back to the conversation.

"I got nothing," I said, with my own smile. "You've pretty much tied it all up. The drugs were taken by this guy in a Move It truck, a common sight in any storage facility. My security system caught him on tape and someone took the tape. That about sum it up?"

John nodded and wiped his mouth. He, too, took a sip of coffee. "Next?"

"Next what?" I pushed my plate to the side.

"The disks. Whoever took the disks is part of this."

"I was afraid you were going to say that."

"I know you were. You also got the part that whoever took the disks has access to not only the units but the office. That sort of narrows it down don't you think?"

"You mean who was in the office?"

"I mean whoever was in the office is probably involved in drugs."

My turn to nod. "That seems obvious. It wasn't me."

John gave me another smile, those chocolate eyes warm as hot fudge. "Never thought it was. Good thing we changed the locks on your front door," he said.

"I think it may be time to change out the others," I said.

"Marlie, listen to me. This isn't a game. I want you to be very careful. Someone has killed two men already. One more won't make a difference."

"There's nothing wrong with me changing the locks," I said. "I should have done it before. Actually that should have been one of the first things I did. The previous managers have keys and who knows how many others they may have given away. Heaven knows Mrs. Murphy must have lost more than the ones I've found."

"Just be careful," John warned again. "You're out there alone. People know that. Stay indoors after dark. Keep the door locked. And watch those cameras when anyone is on the lot."

"All things I've already thought about," I smiled. "I'll be fine, John. I've been there two years without a problem."

"Before," he said. "Like it or not there's something going on there. I hope this is the end of it, I really do." He pushed his plate aside and leaned forward on folded arms. "This guy, Burke. When is he there?"

I shrugged. "Hard to say. He's in and out. He's gone for a few days then he's back. He's back now."

"Where was he?"

"No idea. He never tells me where he's been. He won't even tell me when he's leaving. He just doesn't show up for days and then he's there again. His

133

motorhome is there so if anyone is watching the place, they probably know it."

"His motorhome? He stays there?"

"Part of the time. The idea was for him to watch the place at night. I don't know how that turned out. He never told me anything."

"Did he stay the whole night?"

"Again, I don't know. It's not like I was out there with him."

John laughed. "On a personal note, I'm glad to hear that," he said. "I'll check with him, see if he saw anything. In the meantime, humor me. Stay inside when it gets dark. Don't go wandering out there on your own."

"I appreciate your concern, John, but it's not a bank. It's a storage facility."

"Where drugs were stored, even briefly. Plus a guy seen inside that facility wound up dumped off the freeway with a bullet in his head. I would bet the other guy was with him. Be careful."

John pulled out his wallet and removed a card. "Here. Take my card. My cell phone is on there, too. If you see or hear anything call me. I can be there in fifteen minutes."

I took the card, pretty sure I already had one, and stuck it in my back pocket. "Yes, sir. I have it."

He reached to pat my hand. "That was not an order, Marlie. That was a request. And a polite one." He folded his fingers around mine and gave them a squeeze. "Besides, I like having someone to eat dinner with."

I smiled and tugged my hand loose, picking up my check.

John took it and added it to his. "I got this."

"Thanks for dinner," I said, standing up. "Next time will be on me."

"You have a deal. I'll hold you to that."

On the way home I decided it was okay if these guys wanted to foot the bill for my dinners. At least until I figured out which one was dealing in drugs.

Chapter 14

I had my own plan that I put in effect Tuesday morning. I had the golf cart out at first light, before the gates were open.

When a customer gets behind on their rent it's overlocked with a heavy, bright red lock. When it's in place it makes it impossible to open the unit until it's removed. Customers who manage to tailgate in behind another vehicle still can't get into their units when the red locks are in place. There are two master keys. One is on the keyring clipped to my jeans. The other is in a drawer in the office, in case Steve needs to unlock someone on the weekend.

Tuesday morning I ordered all new red locks, four dozen of them and paid for rush delivery. While I was at it I ordered a dozen of our usual chrome locks only these, too, were keyed alike. One key would open them all.

I intended to replace all those little yellow plastic tabs on the empty units with red locks. Ideally that puts an end to anyone using one of them. It takes a good sized set of bolt cutters to get them off. The locks are all keyed alike and I'm going to have the only key.

An added bonus? No more playing tag with Mrs. Murphy on the vacant units. I suspected she had removed a few of those yellow tags in the past to grab up another unit for her personal use. She was not strong enough to man bolt cutters even if she knew how.

Last night I copied the backup disk when I locked up and took that copy upstairs with me. It now rested in a shoebox on the top shelf of my closet, soon to be joined with tonight's duplicate. New procedure: I would copy all of the disks and take them upstairs, leaving the original filed as usual.

I locked the office after work and was out on the lot again, this time with the extension ladder. Using the ladder I readjusted two cameras, aiming them at the front gate. I wasn't worried about who was coming in. I wanted to know who was going out. The access recorder kept the log of who entered and who left by recording the code used. I wanted to see who was leaving, and when. Tailgating in meant tailgating out. The new angles on the cameras covered the entire drive, not just the control pads. No one was going out that gate without being seen.

Satisfied with my day's work I put the cart up and headed upstairs, carrying the duplicate disk. On my way to the shower I stuck it in the shoe box with its companion.

I completely forgot Burke was bringing dinner. When he knocked I was surprised to see him but happy to see the big brown bag he carried.

"You smell good," he said, passing me and going straight to the kitchen. "I hope Chinese is okay."

"You know it is," I said, following him to the kitchen where he was setting out little white pasteboard boxes. "How was your trip?"

137

He crumbled the brown bag, tossed it in the trash can and gathered me in his arms. "I've missed you," he said, kissing my neck until I backed away. "What's with you? I missed you! Aren't you happy to see me?"

"I am happy to see you, Burke. I'm even happier to see Chinese food," I said, handing him a plate.

He took the plate and turned to the food. "Nice welcome there, Marlie."

"If I'd known you were coming I would have ordered the parade."

He turned and put his hands on his hips. "What is with you?"

I sighed and set down my almost full plate. "What is wrong with you? We're friends, Burke, that's it. Did my life end when you left? No. You've only been gone a week or so. It's not like you were missing for years. What's the big deal?"

He put both hands on the counter and leaned on them, dropping his head. "I'm sorry," he said after a minute. "Been a rough week, I'm tired and I was looking forward to tonight. Maybe a little too much. Let's eat. We can talk later."

"Let's start over," I said, feeling a little guilty.

His head snapped up and his eyes were alight. "At the beach? I'm up for that!"

I hip checked him and shoved him over. "Get out of the way. I'm hungry."

With that he chuckled, moved and we were back to normal.

~~~

138

We ate at the coffee table and watched a movie, comfortable again. When the movie ended I turned off the television. "Now, what's been going on? You said we could talk after dinner."

He shook his head. "You are like a bulldog with a bone, aren't you?"

I sat down on the couch and faced him. "You said we'd talk. So talk."

"Well, let's see. I was in Mexico. Is that what you wanted to know?"

"It's a start. Did that have anything to do with the drugs? The ones found here?"

"Yes and no. I can't give you any details on the investigation. I've been working on this case for over a year. The drugs here? Just a drop in the bucket. Will they come back here? No, I don't think so. I'm pretty sure that was a one-time thing. Anything else?"

Yeah, I thought, a lot of something else. Aloud I said, "You don't think those murdered men were connected to the drugs?"

Burke looked confused. "What murdered men? You lost me."

"The ones along the freeway, the one I thought I had on tape."

"Oh, that. I forgot about that. No, babe, sorry. I don't think that had anything to do with you or the storage facility. Those guys were probably into something, yes. Drug related? Possible. That kind of killing is rarely solved. Those guys were more than likely the brawn, not the brains. They don't fill out an application, babe. Some guy steps up and says rent a truck, drive here, pick up the load and put it here and you make five grand. From what I've seen in the last year half of these guys are high school dropouts or drug burnouts. They want a big payoff for a little work. None of them are master criminals. You're perfectly safe."

Two guys, two different outlooks. "Did you turn in that file I put together? The one with the access printouts and that partial photo?"

"Turn it in to who? I dropped it off in the task force room, or the rooms they're using at the Sheriff's department. I already told you I don't think that was the guy. Don't get me wrong, Marlena. You did a bang up job on that, you did. For an amateur? Great." He reached to pat my hand. "These guys working this case are professionals. This is their job. Some of them, like Miller, have made it a career. That's all he does. Others like the local guy, Kincaid? Not his territory. He's out of his league and he knows it."

"And you?"

Burke took a deep breath and blew it out. "Me? I've been at it too long. This isn't my first case but it may be my last."

"You're quitting?"

"Sure thinking about it," he said. "I see you, come here and have dinner, watch a movie and I want to quit tomorrow. Get a place here in town with you and retire. Get a dog, do a little fishing. Put it all behind me."

"You think you could walk away from it?"

"Oh hell yes," he said. "In a heartbeat. I've been giving it a lot of thought." He turned those warm dark eyes on me and turned up the heat. "Since I met you. If you could cook, I'd marry you tomorrow."

"Oh, I see," I laughed. "Cooking is a prerequisite."

140

He folded his fingers around mine. "In your case? I'll do the cooking."

Where did this come from?

I pulled my hand free and stood up. "I have to work tomorrow and I have a lot to do. My help has been missing," I said, smiling to soften the rebuke. "Time for Burke to go."

He stood up, stretched and headed for the door. "I'm gonna let it go this time, Marlie," he said, curling his hand around my neck. "We're gonna talk about this some more." He tugged me close and kissed me, soft and warm. "Soon."

I stepped back and opened the door. "Thanks again for dinner, Burke."

He brushed against me as he went out. "Soon," he said again and went down the stairs.

I locked the door and listened for his truck. In a few minutes I heard it start and fade down the street.

He wasn't staying out back tonight.

In bed later I thought about what he told me. He was of the opinion it was over, that it was a one hit kind of thing and I had no worries. The dead men were a totally unrelated event. From that he bounced to getting a place with me. Where did that come from? Friends, yes. Flirts? Yes. We had formed a comfortable relationship with a lot of innuendo and casual flirting. From that to getting a place together? I don't think so.

On the other hand John Kincaid warned me to be careful, to take extra precautions, convinced the dead men were connected to both the drugs and the facility. These two worked together, on the task force, yet their views and opinions were opposite ends of the same stick.

Just before I drifted off I thought about Paul Murphy. Did he have a hand on that stick? And where?

Chapter 15

Wednesday Burke was on the lot, broom in hand. I saw him talking to Randy and later helping Mrs. Murphy unload her car. Where that woman found all those books was beyond me.

I read a lot. It's my way of updating my brain's software. The Kindle was my salvation – I didn't have room for boxes of books. My Kindle was loaded with old favorites and those I wanted to read. I loved books. You get the picture.

Mrs. Murphy owned a book store in San Luis Obispo and another in Paso Robles. That woman could remember the name of every book she read, how much it was worth, and made a fortune in collectible books. She sold online as well as out of her stores which she paid someone else to manage. There was not a yard sale, garage sale, rummage sale or estate sale that she didn't attend. Which also explained her need for more storage units, which she didn't pay for as the family owned the facility. The male Murphy's made it clear from day one I was not to give her another unit. So began the game of hide the empties from Mrs. Murphy.

The other side of that particular coin was common courtesy. She was a good deal older than me and there was no way I would sit around and watch her load and unload those heavy cartons of books. Was not going to happen. On her side she expected the help. After all was said and done, she was an owner. She rarely asked anyone for help and always had more than she needed.

Today Burke was within hailing distance and I kinda enjoyed watching him unload her SUV. On the camera I noticed they talked quite a lot and often laughed together.

While Burke was unloading her cartons and carrying them inside the unit I watched her walk up one side of the aisle and come back down the other side. She was looking for another unit. While I watched she reached out and snapped off one of the breakaway yellow tags and stuck it in her pocket. Often suspected and now proven.

That would stop once I had the new locks. For now, I could only watch as she swung the door open and stepped inside. She was back in a minute and walked up to where Burke was leaning on the tailgate of her truck. It didn't take a genius to understand her gestures as she directed him to the open door behind her. Gritting my teeth I watched as he began to carry cartons down there and put them inside.

There is a site map of the entire facility on the wall in the office. We use it to show customers the location of their unit as well as the flow of traffic, the rest room, and the exits.

It's a simple system. The map, mounted on a large cork board, is marked with colored push pins. A green pin means available, a yellow pin means it needs repair. A single glance tells me how many vacancies I have and how many need repairs.

It's faster than using the computer – one look, as opposed to three different screens.

In the office I pulled the green pin out of the unit she had confiscated, signaling it was no longer available and crossed it off the vacancy list. She was allowed one. This was number seven. Papa and Paul were gonna be right in my craw when they found out. My only hope was to head her off.

Burke had taken the cart since he was sweeping back there so I had to lock up the office and hike to where they were. By the time I got there Burke was unloading the last of the cartons. Only one remained in the truck bed.

"Oh, hello Marlena," Mrs. Murphy sang out, her eyes twinkling. "How are you today, my dear?"

"I'm just fine, Mrs. Murphy. You know you're not supposed to remove those tags from the empty units. You'll mess up my system."

Her eyes rounded as she returned my look. "Remove? I didn't remove a thing," she said wide-eyed. "This one had no tag or lock. I only looked inside and saw it was vacant. Don't worry," she smiled, "the boys won't mind."

Like hell, I thought. I stepped around her and went inside the unit. It wasn't as bad as I feared, only a dozen or so boxes lined the wall.

"Mrs. Murphy, I'm sure we can make room in your other unit for these. Let's go take a look."

I headed down the row to the other unit whose door still stood ajar.

Burke sat on the tailgate of her truck, swinging his feet and smiling at me.

"Problem?"

I glared at him with my best stink eye and stepped inside.

The back of the unit and both sides were lined with stacks of cartons, as close together as brick work. Two more rows ran down the center space, stacked two high. To bring the others, I would have to rearrange these to three high.

Stepping back outside, I looked at Burke. "Bring those down here," I said. "Stack them on top of the middle rows."

Burked slid off the tailgate. "She's gonna have a fit you know. She doesn't like to have to shift them when she's looking for something."

"She's gonna have to deal with the men in the family," I said. "My job is on the line. If she gets one more unit, I will be among the unemployed."

"Oh, I doubt that," Burke grinned. "The family is fond of you."

"What is that supposed to mean?"

Burke's eyebrows went up. "Just what I said. The family is fond of you. They like you, Marlie."

"And you would know that how?"

"I told you I know them. I've known them forever. They always speak very highly of you. Especially Paul."

Was that a dig? I wondered what Paul had told Burke.

"It's still my job," I said. "Give me a hand and we'll move those back up here." I turned around and went back to the other unit where Mrs. Murphy was standing with her hands on her hips.

"What are you doing?" She asked as I grabbed the first carton and headed the other way. "Those go in here. You're going to get them all mixed up."

Ignoring her, I kept going, lugging the carton of books towards her unit.

"Look here, Missy," she called after me. I heard her footsteps coming my way.

I kept going, stepping inside and setting the carton on top of another in her center row. By the time I turned to the door she was waiting for me.

"I asked you what you think you're doing."

"Mrs. Murphy, you know the guys don't want you to have another unit. That unit is being held for a nice young couple coming in today. These will fit fine in here. Burke and I will move them for you, it's not a problem."

She stomped a tiny, sneakered foot. "It is a problem, young lady! I own this place and I will put my things where I want. If you don't like it you can lump it."

I counted to ten and began to organize my argument when another voice joined in.

"Something wrong, mom?"

I turned to see Paul getting out of his car. Things getting better and better. Maybe it was time for me to look for another job after all. These people were nuts and I was getting tired of it.

"Paulie!" She scurried around me and went to throw her arms around her son. "I haven't seen you in ages. Why haven't you come by the house? Do I have to make an appointment to see you?"

"Whoa, mom, slow down," he said, returning her hug. "It's been busy, you know that. Now, what's going on? The office is locked and no one is around." He looked at me. "Is there a problem?"

"We're just moving some cartons for your mother," I said. "She's downsizing, as you told her. We're moving those boxes into this one and that will free up a unit for rental."

He hugged his mother again. "Good job, Mom! The old man will be proud of you. Let's go tell him. I'll treat you to lunch as a reward. What do you say?"

I managed not to smirk. Now it was her turn to simmer.

"I'd love that, Paulie. Come on, let's go. They can finish up here without me." Turning to me her eyes went cold. "Don't mix up those cartons with these. Put these on top of those and then make a new row for the new ones. They have to be kept separate." She stepped inside and gestured to the center rows. With ease she picked up the carton I had just set on top of the row and put it aside. "This is one of the new ones. I want it in a new row. These can be stacked up together. Then make a new row with the others. Do you understand? Shall I draw you a diagram?"

"Thank you, Mrs. Murphy," I answered. "I've got it."

"Well, then, get it done. I'm going to lunch with my son but I will be back to check that you've done it correctly."

With that she snaked her arm through Paul's and smiled up at him. "Where are we going for lunch? Do you want to go to San Luis? It's a lovely day for a drive and we haven't seen each other in ages."

He opened the car door for her and helped her inside. "Can't do it today, mom. Too busy at work. How about Kelly's? Or The Hatch? You like the fish and chips there."

Mrs. Murphy slid into the seat and clipped the seat belt. "You can choose," she smiled. "Whatever you would like." Then she looked at me. "I'll be back to check on those cartons so you be careful how you line them up."

"I will," I answered. "I'll be very careful." Time to get my resume ready. Again.

Paul winked at me before he slid behind the wheel and started the car. He mouthed 'don't worry' as he drove by us. His mother didn't bother to wave.

"That went well," Burke said from the tailgate, where he still sat swinging his legs.

"How would you like to kiss my pearly pink fanny," I said, starting back to the other unit.

"I would love it," he said behind me. "Thought you'd never ask."

My temper was enough to fuel moving the cartons out of the unit and returning it to its empty state. When the move was complete I grabbed a red over lock from the cart and locked the empty one. No more yellow tags.

I checked inside her unit to be sure things were as she ordered before relocking it. Looking around for her lock I saw it on the ground the other side of her car. Sparkling in the sun were her keys, one still stuck in the lock. I sighed, picked them up, locked her unit and took a seat on the cart, dangling the key ring.

Burke leaned in and kissed me, his lips warm on mine. "You handled that nicely," he said. "Shove over, I'll drive."

I slid over and he got in and turned on the cart.

"Why didn't you stop her?" I asked when we were headed for the office.

"Me? I don't work here, remember? I can't tell anyone what to do. I am strictly an observer. And a sweeper." He grinned at me. "And a dinner companion."

I sighed again. "You seemed to know her."

"I do know her. I've known Colleen for a long time. I told you. I went to school with Paul."

"Do you know the parents of every kid you went to school with?"

"No. I don't." He made the turn and pushed the remote to open the gates. "Paul and I spent a lot of time together in school. Same teams, that kind of thing. I got to know his parents. When I'm in town I always go by and say hello."

Back at the office a couple was waiting for me so I went to work. Burke walked back to the lot. While I was showing and renting the unit we had just emptied the UPS truck dropped off three cartons.

The new locks arrived.

Mrs. Murphy's car was still in the back so her return was assured. I didn't want to share the lock switch idea so I lugged the new cartons into the kitchen. Grateful for a strong back after moving boxes of books and locks all morning I made a pot of coffee and got out the Kindle.

It was the fourteenth, a slow time of the month and I was grateful as I carried my coffee to the counter. One page into the story and Burke came in the front door and took a seat at the counter.

"You got around the old lady this morning," he said first thing. "You think she's gonna rat you out?"

I set the Kindle aside. "For what? Taking away that unit? Who cares? I'm about done with this job anyway."

"Whoa, babe, that sounds serious. What's wrong? You don't think they'll really fire you, do you? No way. They like you, I told you that. Paul saw what was going on. Besides, who's gonna run this place if you leave? Papa and Paul don't have time and heaven knows Trick isn't about to do it."

I sighed. "I like the job, Burke. I like it a lot. It's a case of too many roosters and not enough hens. Although the one hen I have is a handful. I don't need the job. I have options."

"Did something else happen? While I was gone?"

Did I want to tell him about Paul? No, they were friends. "It's an easy job," I said. "Most of the customers are nice, they don't spend a lot of time here. Not like working in a store, where there's people all the time."

"You don't like people?"

I shook my head. "Not especially. I'm comfortable on my own. This job gives me a lot of time to myself. I like that."

"I'd hate it," Burke said with a smile. "I like people, like having them around."

"Different strokes," I said.

"How come you're single, Marlie? You're a good looking woman. I know for a fact you're warm and responsive, so how come there's no Mr. Marlie hanging around?"

"I've been a Mrs. It didn't take."

"Aha, thereby hangs the tail. What happened?"

"No big deal, Burke. It didn't work out so we called it quits."

He shifted forward, leaning on his folded arms. "I repeat, what happened? You're beautiful, smart and funny. What didn't he like?"

"You assume he left," I said. "Other way around."

Burke considered me, his brown eyes warm, a half smile on his face. "Marlie, any man you gave your heart to would be a fool to let you go. What happened? Did he find someone else?"

I took a deep breath and blew it out. "You want to know? Okay. He liked outdoor sports too much. So I left and filed for divorce. End of story."

"Outdoor sports? That makes no sense at all," Burke scoffed. "Like hiking or fishing? What kind of outdoor sports?"

"Bob and Jack and Steve. You want me to continue?"

It took a minute for Burke to get it. When he did he patted my hand. "Give it another chance, babe. You are not built to live alone."

I laughed. "Is that an invitation?"

"No," he said quickly. "Not what I meant." Then he saw my smile and sat back. "Not that I wouldn't accept one if you put it out there."

I smiled at Burke. "I'm over it, Burke. Have been for quite a while. I appreciate your concern for my social status but I'm good with it. I'm comfortable. I can stay up late or go to bed early, I eat what I want when I want, I don't have to worry about someone else and I control the channel changer."

"Is that why you reject my advances?"

I laughed again. "What advances, Burke? I'm not an idiot, although sometimes I wonder about that, too. You're a good looking man, and you know it. You have a great personality. You are also doing a very dangerous job, one that takes you all over and I think you enjoy that part, the travel. You're not the kind of guy to settle down."

"You might be surprised," he said softly. "You don't know the real me."

"Okay," I nodded. "Let me put it this way. The 'you' I know, and like by the way, is a handsome, warm, funny guy whose company I enjoy. You know that. For me, that's good enough. I don't want anything more."

He considered that for a minute, his eyes wandering over my face. "I think you do," he said softly, almost a whisper. "We'll see who's right." He stood up and pulled out his keys. "I have a meeting this afternoon. See you later?"

"I'll be here," I said.

He left and I went to the cameras. Mrs. Murphy's car still sat in aisle two.

I wanted to get the new locks on right away but I didn't want Mrs. M. to catch me. She would find out soon enough. I had planned to do it after the gates closed. If Burke was going to be around I didn't want him to catch me either. With a sigh I decided to put the locks off another day. I busied myself making a list of the empty units in numerical order, to speed up the process.

It was almost closing time when I saw Paul drive through the gate. He dropped his mother at her car and left immediately. I got her keys, got the cart and took them out to her. She was digging around in her purse when I reached her.

I stopped the cart and climbed out, holding the keys over my head. "I found them," I called, approaching the car. "You dropped them."

She turned and gave me a sour look. "I did not drop them," she said. "You must have forgotten to give them back when you moved those books. Well, open it up. I want to be sure you did as I instructed."

I used her keys to unlock the unit, holding the door for her.

"Tell me again why I don't have lights in here," she said, stepping inside.

"You have lights in your large unit. The boys put them in for you."

"That's right," she nodded. "And I don't have them here because?"

"You'll have to check with the boys, ma'am. I think it had something to do with the wiring."

"I'll tell Patrick to fix it," she said, doing a turn. "I can't work in this gloom. I want to see that other unit. Maybe the light is better in there."

"I'm so sorry, I rented that unit this afternoon. I told you it was taken."

She put a manicured hand on her hip. "Why would you do that? You knew I wanted that one."

154

"I get paid to rent the units. A man called this morning, wanting that size."

"I want one that size. On that side of the aisle. The light will be better."

"Yes, ma'am, I'll put your name on the list."

"The list? That was the only large one available?"

"Yes ma'am."

"I'll talk to the boys," she smiled and held out her hand for her keys. I handed them to her and watched as she got in her car and left, leaving the unit door wide open and the lock on the ground.

I locked up and went back to the office. Closing time was not coming fast enough.

The cart carries more than passengers. There's several brooms, dust pans and trash bags, along with a box of tools. Another box contains the red overlocks and the yellow tags as well as oil spray and graphite for sticky locks.

Back at the office I spent the remainder of the afternoon with the new locks and a black permanent marker. We use the circular locks, the ones with the keyhole in the center. They are the best in the business when it comes to storage lockers – sturdy, short hasp and very hard to cut, even with the diamond bit drill they are hard to get off.

The new ones were identical to the old ones, a duplicate of a previous order. Using the black marker I drew a small circle around the key hole, just outside of the chrome. No one would notice unless they laid the old and the new side by side. I marked both the red and the chrome. When they were all marked I loaded them on the cart and went out to do my rounds.

At every empty unit I pulled off the yellow tab and replaced it with two locks, one red and one chrome. The unit now looked like all the other overlocks – a customer's lock overlocked with a bright red one. The difference being these chrome locks were also mine. I could unlock and remove both when I rented the unit.

At a glance, the empty units were now camouflaged.

Fortunately Mrs. Murphy rarely came into the office, usually she just pulled up to the unit she wanted and honked. Or waved at the camera on her way in and I followed her in the cart. She was accustomed to having someone load or unload for her and she was entitled. She was an owner and a lady of a certain age older than my own. Had she ever used the map she could have driven to every empty unit in the facility by reading the green pins.

Satisfied with my day's work I added one more trick before I went upstairs. I snipped a couple of hairs, licked my fingers, and stuck them across both front and back doors.

If someone opened either door I would know.

~~~

First thing Thursday I checked the doors and found both the little hairs still in place. I lifted them carefully and set them aside to be reused. I might not catch anyone with this childish trap but I would know if someone was prowling around at night.

Next up was changing the door locks. I did the back door first, then followed that with the door to the garage, leaving the front door last. Of course the minute I got both door knobs out Patrick Murphy drove up.

"Hey, Red," he called as he walked up to the door. "What'cha up to?"

My cheeks warmed up although I avoided a full blown blush. "Good afternoon," I said. "What can I do for you?"

He shoved his hands in his back pockets and grinned at me. "More like what I can do for you." He stood close and looked at the hole in the front door where the knobs used to be. "Gonna be hard to lock like that," he said. "You gonna just tie it with a bungee cord?"

I dusted my hands on my jeans. "I have new ones, right there on the desk."

He looked first, then went over and lifted the plastic blister pack. "This gonna fit? Did you measure it first?"

I hoped he didn't hear my eyes roll. "Yes, sir, I did." I took the package from him and pried it open with the screwdriver, careful not to drop the hardware pack of screws.

Patrick turned back to the door and squatted in front of it. "Hand me that screwdriver," he said.

I did as he asked and watched as he ran it around the inside of the cutout hole. When that was done he held out his hand, palm up.

"What?"

"Give me the knobs, the lock."

I handed over the parts to the door and watched as he matched them, checked them and inserted them through the hole in the door.

Like a surgeon he said, "Screwdriver" and I handed it over. In minutes he had the new doorknobs installed.

Standing, he looked at me. "Key?"

I handed him one of the two and twisted the other onto my keyring.

He cocked an eyebrow at me before he tried the key. He fiddled with it, checking it out both open and closed, then closed it and turned back to me. He held the key up and dangled it in front of me. "Is this for me?"

For no earthly reason I blushed. I felt the heat climbing my neck and turned away. Too late. Patrick's robust laugh filled the office, making my ears flame.

"That is the damnedest thing I have seen in a long time," he said with a wide smile. "You are the first woman I have seen blush since third grade when my teacher walked into the boys bathroom by mistake."

"I'm so happy I amuse you," I said. "It's not like I do it on purpose."

He was instantly serious, his brows gathering over those bright blue eyes. "Hey, lady, I was teasing you. Lighten up. It's a compliment."

"Sorry," I said.

"Let me start over. Is this key for me?"

And I blushed again, the heat filling my face. I looked up to see him trying not to laugh, his eyes dancing as he clamped his lips closed.

I took a deep breath and looked at me feet, counting to ten.

"I'll have duplicates made for the family," I said, holding out a palm for the key he held.

He folded his fingers around the key and palmed it. "I can do that," he said and stuck the key in the pocket of his jeans. "How about the back door? Do we need to change that out, too?"

I shook my head. "No, I already did those, both the back door and the door to the garage."

He looked at me and the laughter was gone, his eyes cold and intent. "Why?"

"Why what?"

"Why are you changing all the locks? Is there a problem? Something I should know?"

"It's a preventative measure," I answered. "I should have done it when I first started here. No telling how many of the old keys are floating around. I'll have the new ones copied and see that you have them."

He held his palm out. "I told you I'd do that. Where are the others?"

I went around the counter to the desk drawer and pulled out the envelope where I had put the other keys. I handed it to him.

He felt through the paper and looked at me. "There's only two keys?"

"One for each door," I said. "Do you want me to mark them for you?"

"No need for that. Are these the only keys? The new locks came with only one key?"

"No, sir. I have one of each," I patted the key ring on my belt.

He considered me for a couple of minutes. "Those are the only others?"

"Yes, sir. Each lock came with two keys. I have one and you now have the others."

"Sir is my father. My name is Patrick."

I nodded again.

"Can you say that?"

"Yes, Patrick, I can say it. Is there anything else?"

"Well," he drew his brows down and frowned at me. "Actually, Miss Montoya, you could do something for me."

"Yes, sir," I said and bit my tongue. "Patrick," I amended. "What can I do for you?"

"Blush," he said with a grin.

And I did.

I felt the flush climbing up my neck, all the way to my hairline.

Patrick laughed long and loud, the sound filling the office. He almost stopped once, then looked at me and was off again. He laughed until his eyes were moist and he had to wipe them.

I went over to my desk and sat down, waiting for the hilarity to end.

He came to the counter and sat across from me.

"I am so sorry," he said. "I can't resist. I'll try not to do it again." He said, then his lips quivered. "Red." He was off again, another rolling belly laugh.

My cheeks flamed and I spun around in the chair to look out the window.

He chuckled, snorted, laughed and gasped for another five minutes while I watched the hummingbirds dive bomb the feeder outside the window.

Another minute passed before I heard him move. When I heard the front door open I chanced a look at him.

He was sober and looked contrite. "I'll get these keys duped this afternoon. How many do you need?"

"I have all I need," I said. "You'll need keys for your dad and your brother."

"What about the weekend guy? Won't he need copies?"

Did I want Steve to have copies? I hadn't decided on that yet, assuming he could use mine. "Yes, I guess," I said. "One of each."

Patrick opened the door and looked at me for another long minute. "I'll have them tomorrow," he said. "Red." His laugh followed him like the tail of a kite.

I said some really rude, unkind words under my breath and kicked the trash can before closing up and heading home. Luckily for them, none of the guys crossed my path that night. It was peanut butter and jelly, a hot shower and an early night with the Kindle.

Chapter 16

Have you ever had one of those days when you wake up, stretch and give thanks for weekends only to find out it's Friday? Welcome to my world. I was half way through my shower when it hit me that I had another work day on my plate.

That start on the day can only go downhill. Finding Paul Murphy parked in front of the office was proof.

I unlocked the front door, turned the sign to 'Open' and went to my desk to boot up the computer. I heard Paul's truck door slam before I got to my chair. Sitting, I pasted on my ten cent smile and greeted him.

"Morning, Marlie," he said. "How are you this fine day?"

"Glad it's Friday," I said. "Can I help you with something?"

"Yeah, you can explain why my key to the front door doesn't work. Something I should know?" He leaned on the counter with both hands.

"I changed out the locks. Patrick is getting the new keys copied for you. He said he'd have them today."

"Trick? How did he get them? Has he been hanging around here?"

I shook my head. "No, sir. He helped finish installing the new door knobs yesterday afternoon. He volunteered to get the keys duplicated," I explained, while wondering why he was trying to get in the office. "Is there something you needed?"

"Yeah, I need this week's deposit records. Stay put, I can get them," he said, going into the back office. I heard him rustling around for a few minutes. He came out carrying a manila file folder. "I copied these so you can keep the originals."

"Okay. Do you still want me to email the week's totals?"

"Monday as usual. I wanted to get an idea of how we're doing this month. I'll talk to Trick about those keys. In the future, you work for me. I am your supervisor. You want to change locks, you clear it with me first."

"Yes, sir. I didn't know it was necessary. I should have changed the locks when I first took the job. The other managers might have copies, they might have forgotten to turn them all in. With the recent problems I thought it was a necessary move."

Paul looked at me and nodded. "You're right, we should have done that when the other managers left. They weren't the most reliable people. I should have thought of it. It's all right this time. Just remember in the future, run anything like this past me first."

"I will. I didn't realize I needed permission."

"Like you said, with recent events around here it brings me up a little short when I'm locked out of my own business. I apologize if I was rude. You can understand my concern."

"No need to apologize," I smiled. "You are the boss. I'll remember to check with you on any changes in the future."

"How's Burke? I haven't seen him around."

"I assume he's all right. He was on the lot the other day."

"He's still hanging around here?"

"Yes, sir."

"Has he found anything? Heard anything?"

"You'd have to ask him. He doesn't report to me," I said.

"That right? I thought you two were an item," he smiled.

I took a breath before I answered. "We're friends."

"With benefits?" His smirk looked oily, his eyes half closed as he watched my face.

"Mr. Murphy, sir. We have had this conversation before. If you are unhappy with my job performance fire me. Otherwise, I have work to do."

He tossed me a smile that made me want another shower. "I was just teasing you, Marlie. Don't be so sensitive. You're like family to us. I didn't mean to upset you."

"You didn't upset me, Paul. It's Friday and I have a lot of work to do. If there's nothing else I'll get to it."

"It's Friday, take it easy. Close up early if you want, take the afternoon off."

"Thanks, I might do that," I said with no intention of following through.

"Well, you have a nice day."

"You too."

With that he left and I heard his truck start. When I couldn't hear it any more I went into the kitchen and washed my hands and face before making a pot of coffee. I was either going to quit or talk to Papa Murphy again. I didn't like that idea at all.

On the plus side I knew who was in the office when I wasn't around. Paul had all that information he was supposed to be looking for on his desk. I sent it over every Monday morning. He lied about his purpose in the office. What else had he lied about? One little check mark for Mr. Paul.

Around lunch time Mrs. Murphy pulled up at the gate and honked. I waved from the window, put the 'Manager Outside, Please Wait' sign on the door and locked the office. By the time I got the cart and drove out to her unit she was fumbling around with the lock.

I took her keys, opened the unit and handed them back to her. "Good morning, Mrs. M, how are you today?"

"Wonderful," she trilled. "I found so many good books today! And some wonderful antique glass. And I still have to go to the church rummage sale tomorrow. It's a very good week for me."

She seemed to be past me taking away the unit yesterday. "Can I help you unload?"

Beaming, she lifted the hatchback of the SUV and stood aside. "If you would be so kind, I would appreciate it. Those boxes get heavier as the day goes on. I think the sun swells them or something."

The back was filled with boxes of books. I smiled at her and picked up the closest one. "Are we putting them in the same rows as yesterday?"

With a frown she stepped inside the unit and put her hands on her hips. "I have to have more room. This is not acceptable. I can't work in here! I want some more space."

All the time she complained I was standing holding the heavy carton. "Where do you want this one?" I had my own suggestion but kept it to myself.

Her sigh could have been heard in town. "Just stack them right there by the door. I'm going to talk to the boys," she said, rattling her keys. "What good is it to own a storage facility if you can't use it? Am I right?"

Oh, boy. Not taking sides in this one. "Let me get these unloaded for you," I said, ignoring her question. I set down the carton I was holding and went back for another. Mrs. M. wandered to the center row of cartons and opened up the nearest one. Those we had unloaded yesterday. No complaints from the lady.

I worked as fast as I could, feeling my back muscles stretch out as I made trip after trip, from the car to the unit and back. The last boxes were tight against the back of the front seat and I had to crawl inside the cabin to tug them back so I could get a grip on them. I pulled them along while I backed out so I wouldn't have to crawl in here again. My knees were right at the hinge, my feet hanging out in space as I tugged them back.

A wolf whistle split the air and I jumped, banging my head on the roof of the car. Cuss words danced on my tongue as I backed the rest of the way out and got to my feet. I turned around to meet the happy smile of Patrick Murphy.

"Nice view there, Red," he grinned before his mother threw her arms around his neck.

"Patrick! I am so happy to see you," she squealed like a girl. "Come here and look at this," she said, tugging on his hand.

He followed along but his head was turned toward me and I saw his wink.

I pulled the next carton out and froze.

Like the other cartons this one was filled with books. Wedged in willy-nilly were several dozen hard cover books. The spaces between were filled with paperbacks. The books didn't get my attention. The carton did.

Old sealing tape covered both sides, one end dangling loose at the seam. Packing tape with the distinctive red, green and white fibers reinforcing it. The Christmas tape. I had seen it before. On cartons of drugs.

I could hear Mrs. M. telling Patrick about the need for more space. A quick glance told me they were inside the unit, away from the door. I pulled out my cell phone and took a couple of shots of the carton and its tape. With the phone jammed back in my pocket I lifted the box and carried it inside.

Mrs. M. was in high gear now, listing the reasons she needed more space.

I glanced at Patrick. He rolled his eyes before looking to heaven for an answer. I smiled in spite of myself.

He stepped over and took the carton from me. "I've got it," he said. "Let me do this. I'm sure you have better things to do."

"Thank you," I said and meant it. "If you need any more help, just holler."

As soon as I cleared the door I jogged back to the cart and headed for the office.

The question now was who do I show the photos to?

In the office I sent the images on my phone to my email address giving me copies if I needed them. I would figure out who to send them to after I had time to think about it.

An hour later Mrs. Murphy left and her son made for the office.

Patrick came in and went around the counter straight to the map of the facility on the wall behind me.

"Can I help you?"

That's asking for it, I thought, too late.

With one eyebrow raised he looked at me. "Well, yeah, you can," he grinned. "The question is will you?" Those damnable blue eyes sparkled. I expected one of those cartoon stars to twinkle in them any minute.

I felt the warmth in my cheeks and started counting to ten. "Let's try that again," I said. "Is there something I can do for you?" Stepped in my own trap.

He laughed and turned to face me. "You are a trip, Red. You're more fun than puppies."

I kept my mouth shut.

Still chuckling Patrick put out a hand and ruffled my hair. "How about I give you one apology now and it lasts for the rest of the year?"

"No need," I said. "What are you looking for?"

"I hear you caught a rat."

I wasn't sure what he was talking about so I kept my mouth shut.

"Paul came looking for keys this morning."

"I told him you were getting the duplicates."

"He told me." He nodded and looked at the map.

"What's the biggest unit we have?"

I joined him in front of the map. "This one," I pointed. "It's really four units in one. The dividing walls were never built."

"What's in there now?"

"Your mother."

"She has this one, too? How many does she have?"

I tapped the units as I listed them. "The big one, plus this, this and this."

He considered. "She has the company locks? You can open them?"

I nodded.

He scanned the map again, right to left.

I waited.

"How often is she here? Is there a pattern?"

"It varies. Usually it's Mondays and Fridays but it can be any time. Kind of depends on how many yard sales and rummage sales she hits on the weekend. Neptune week and Mardi Gras she's in and out every day, getting things for her shops."

Patrick scrubbed a hand over his face and sighed. "All right," he said. "Let me think about it. I'll see if we can't compact her down some. She spreads her stuff out, takes more room than she needs." He tapped the largest unit. "We need to move all of her stuff in here, see if we can empty out these other units. If we can get it all in here we can repack and restack her stuff, see how much space we can gain. Then we start backing her up," he tapped the map. "Keep condensing her stuff, getting her to move it out or get rid of some of it. After that, we put up another wall, pen her in. What do you think?"

"It'll work," I said. "Unless she catches you at it." I couldn't help but smile at the thought. "Then you're gonna be a big fish in a little bitty bucket." I looked up to see him smiling back at me.

"You have a nice smile. You should smile more often," he said. He waited a minute. "You're getting used to me. No blush. That's a shame."

Shaking my head I turned my back and sat down at my desk.

"I'm on the record," Patrick said behind me. "I already apologized for the rest of the year. I'm not due again till January."

I heard him before he came into view, moving around the counter and heading for the front door. He paused there and looked at me. "We'll get on that next week. I'll see you then." With a wink he left, shutting the door behind him.

The door opened immediately. John Kincaid came in, looking back over his shoulder. "Who was that?"

"Patrick Murphy."

"Ah, the bachelor," he grinned. "Heard a lot about him, never met him." He came to the counter. "Good morning. You have a few minutes?"

"Of course." Now it was down to a game of who do you trust? I had to make a decision. "How long have you been here?"

"Maybe four minutes. Why?"

"I meant in the area," I smiled at him.

"Little over two years. Why?"

Decision made. "I have something to show you." The Murphy family, Paul and Patrick, and friend Declan Burke had been in Monarch for decades. John was relatively new. If someone or two was dealing in drugs it stood to reason it would be someone familiar with the area.

I pulled my phone out of my pocket and thumbed through the photos. I found the ones I wanted and held out the phone.

"What's this?"

"Pictures I just took. Couple of them."

Kincaid looked at the phone, turned it, and tapped the screen to enlarge the photo. Looking up at me he said, "This is a box of books."

"Look at the tape. On the sides."

He looked at the phone and back at me. "It's a box of books with tape on the side."

I shook my head and pointed. "That tape. It's unusual. See the little red strings in the tape?"

He looked again at the phone. "It's reinforced. Standard packing tape."

"Not standard, no. The red thread, and the green and white is rare. It's not quite so apparent on that picture because the screen is so small. I had never seen it until a few weeks ago."

He waited.

"On the cartons," I said.

He waited for me to explain.

With a sigh, I took my phone back. "The cartons with the drugs. This same tape was on them. Taped pretty close to the same way, those side bands on each, three rows of tape both ways."

"Show me again," he said.

I thumbed back to the photos and handed him the phone.

Now he took the time to really look at the photos. "You sure?"

"Yep. I noticed the tape the first time. Thought about getting some for the holidays, because of the colors. The red, green and white."

"Be right back," he said, handing me my phone. He went outside.

He was gone for a while so I went back to work, getting the week's reports ready.

I hoped I hadn't made a mistake, showing him the photos. Maybe the fact that John had a shorter history with the town wasn't important.

Maybe I should have gone to Agent Miller, who had no ties at all to Monarch.

The detective came back inside, smiling.

"Correct," he said. "Good job."

I smiled back, proud of myself. I avoided wiggling like a puppy.

"Can you email those pictures to Miller?" He slid a card across the counter. "This address. He's waiting."

I pulled out my phone again and did as he asked.

"The burning question is where did you find this carton?"

"In Mrs. Murphy's car. I unloaded it earlier. It's in her unit right now."

The detective mulled it over. "You have a key?"

"I do."

"Let's go take a look." He doubled patted the counter.

I locked up the office, got the cart and drove him back to the unit. Inside I showed him the carton in question, having put it on top of a stack.

"Is there a light in here?"

"Nope. Fire hazard. Some people fill these units right to the ceiling. Next to a light bulb? Could be a problem. No lights."

"Never thought about it," he said, pulling out his keys. A mini Maglite flared. He ran it along the strip of packing tape. "What about fingerprints? Worth a shot?"

"I know I handled it, so did Patrick. I assume Mrs. Murphy did, or whoever put it in her car. She reuses boxes all the time, so no telling who handled it before her. You could ask her but I doubt she'd remember."

John straightened and turned off the flashlight, tucking his keys back in his pocket. "It's a lead but I have no idea where it goes," he said after a while. He took a couple of pictures of the carton from different angles. "All right, Marlie, close it back up. Can you keep any eye on this unit?"

"I can. One of our cameras is at the end of the aisle. No problem."

"If they move this carton I want to know."

"I'll let you know," I said, "I don't watch it constantly but the recorder should pick up anyone moving boxes out. Might be hard to tell which carton is which. The cameras aren't that good."

"Do what you can," he said. "In the meantime I'll talk to Miller and the rest of the team."

Oh, boy. Not what I wanted to hear. I was already knee deep in the creek so I might as well swim. "Is there any way you can say you saw the carton? Leave me out of it?"

His head whipped up. "Problem?"

I'm in it now. "I think it might be."

"The owners? Your job? Talk to me, girl."

I took a deep breath and blew it out. "I didn't tell Burke. Or show him. I only showed it to you."

"Why?"

I locked the unit and drove us back to the office, giving myself some time to think. In the office John sat at the counter and folded his arms. "What's the deal with Burke? Is he bothering you?"

How do I answer that? "No, not exactly."

John leaned back and looked at me.

"Okay, here's the thing," I said. "I like Burke. We're friends. Sort of."

"How about you start at the beginning, Marlie? What's going on?"

"All right," I sighed. "I would appreciate it if this was between us?"

He leaned forward again. "You can trust me, Marlena. I'll keep anything you tell me in confidence. Unless it's illegal," he smiled. "I am an officer of the law."

"I know," I said. "This may not even be important."

"Burke?"

"Here we go," I said, more to myself than John, and told him the whole story, from the beach and my first meeting with Burke. I glossed over the kissing part but included the threat with the comb. I brought him up to date with Paul, the incident at Kelly's. He had seen that one. It took a while, even in the abridged version. When

I finished the story I left John to think about it and went to make a fresh pot of coffee. I hoped I had not made a mistake.

Returning with two full mugs I set one in front of him and sat back down.

"Well?"

It was John's turn. "I have a few questions," he admitted.

"Just a few? I did better than I thought," I said and smiled.

He smiled back. "Okay, then. When you met him, the overlook at the beach. Did he ever identify himself as a cop?"

"No."

"These guys that were chasing him. Had you ever seen them before? Or since?"

I shook my head.

"Burke did threaten you, though."

"With a comb," I said.

"Implied threat is still a felony. Terrorism. Burke knows that."

"I was never in danger. When the other guys left he showed me the comb and apologized. Explained a little. Under normal circumstances I would never have seen him again. The whole thing was a fluke. He's an undercover cop, following the drugs. The drugs brought him here. He had no idea I was here, too. Returning my sweatshirt was just Burke, being Burke. Kind of letting me know he was around before he had to identify himself."

"He could have simply come to the office and identified himself," John said. "No need for the dramatics. Unless he had other ideas." He looked at me.

"About me? I never saw the guy before the beach. If it wasn't for the drugs I still wouldn't be seeing him."

"Come on. You're a beautiful woman. I'm sure you've dealt with advances before. Have you considered maybe Burke is interested in more than the drugs?"

"Burke and I are friends, buddies. We like the same foods, we like old movies and I like his company. He's fun to be with. Nothing more. Contrary to what Paul thinks, I have never slept with Burke."

"Your relationship with Burke is platonic. That right?"

"Exactly."

"Okay, that's your view. What about his?"

"What do you mean?"

"Does Burke want more? A romantic relationship?"

That slowed me down. I took time to consider my answer. "Burke is a clown, the class cutup. He's rarely serious."

"That's not an answer, Marlie. Is Burke interested in you?"

I sighed again. At least I knew I was getting enough oxygen. "I don't think so. He jokes about it, teases me about it, but no. When it comes right down to it, no. He's the eternal playboy. I would bet he has more than one female companion."

"You're not one of them."

I shook my head. "No. We're pals, John. That's the end of it. He's here a lot, on the job. He hates to eat alone and he loves old movies. We hang out. That's it."

"How about Paul? Have you had trouble with him?"

"That one incident at Kelly's and you were there for that."

"I remember. Don't take this wrong okay? Do you think maybe Burke is just tweaking Paul's nose? Maybe stretching the truth a little bit?"

"About me? Why? Why would he do that?"

"For some men it's a game. If those two have always been competitive it could have started out like that. Paul could have made a remark and Burke jumped on it. Or vice versa."

"No, I don't see it," I said. "That is completely off base. Paul is married. He's never come on to me in all the time I've worked here. Two years."

John smiled. "So why the sudden interest? It didn't come up until he found Burke in your place that morning. Maybe you're the new prize."

"They're grown men," I said. "That's silly."

John chuckled. "Grown men are often silly, Marlie. I see that all the time." He took a small spiral notebook out of this shirt pocket and thumbed through it. When he found a new page he took a pen from the cup on the counter. "The new locks. Was that because of Burke? Or Paul?"

"Neither. It was because I don't like the idea of someone prowling around down here. Especially at night. I live here."

"Well, you fixed that," he smiled.

"Yeah, and this morning, first thing I have Paul wanting to know why his key didn't work."

That got John's attention. "This morning? When did you change them?"

"Yesterday. Patrick was here and he helped. He has the duplicate keys. He was going to get them copied today for Paul and his dad."

"Patrick? The younger brother?"

"Yes."

"Is he here a lot?"

I shook my head. "I actually just met him. He's been here, on the lot, helping his folks but never came in, introduced himself or anything."

John tapped his chin with the pen. "Is the family close?"

"I guess so. I know the boys adore their mom, do anything they can for her. Paul and his dad are close. Don't know about Patrick and his dad. I assume he would be the same."

"How about the brothers? They close?"

"Don't know. Like I said, I just met Patrick myself."

"What's your take on him?"

"From what I've heard, he's the catch of the county. Permanent bachelor playing the field."

John lifted an eyebrow, asking a question.

"I've had no trouble with him," I said. "He teases me. That's the only personal dealing I've had with him."

"In what way does he tease you?"

"I blush," I said. "It's not my fault. For some reason Patrick finds that funny. He goes out of his way to see if he can make me blush."

178

John smiled and made a note. "Anything off color? Out of line?"

Again I shook my head. "No, not really. General teasing. I'm already getting used to it. Helps me keep from blushing. It'll wear off. Always does."

"I gather you've had this problem for a while?"

"Since I was a child. I inherited my mother's fair skin. I blush easily. I'll get used to him. When I do, no blush."

"Well, I can't arrest him for teasing. Anything else?"

I sighed. "I told you I may be way off base. Something just doesn't add up. What are the odds? Burke is a cop, working undercover with the DEA tracking drugs. One shipment of those drugs winds up in a storage facility owned by Paul, a friend of Burke's going back to high school. Mrs. Murphy comes in with a carton that has the same packing tape as the cartons containing drugs. Someone is coming in and out of the office after hours. Too many connections."

"I agree," he said. "Thank you."

"For what?"

"Trusting me," he smiled. "With Burke a cop, and Paul your boss, you're kind of stuck in the middle." He leaned to take my hand and squeeze it. "For the record, I'm a good cop. I am no relation to any of the parties involved. Only time will prove that, Marlie. And it will. I promise you."

I returned his smile and relaxed. "Do you think I'm nuts?"

"No, I don't. Who's doing what to who may take a while to figure out but I will figure it out. Right now, there's no proof of any wrong doing."

"What about those men? The ones who were killed?"

"I didn't say there was no wrong doing, I said there was no proof. I don't believe in coincidence. Let me run some background checks, see what I can find. In the meantime, I'll notify the task force about the tape on Mrs. Murphy's carton." He looked into my eyes. "My report will say I noticed it and had you open the unit so I could take pictures. That's close to the truth. I'll keep your name out of it as long as I can. Fair enough?"

"Thank you. I appreciate that."

"One more thing. Did Patrick get the keys duplicated?"

"I think so. Patrick said Paul hunted him down for his."

"Paul tried to get in the office last night and his key didn't work. Did he say why he wanted in?"

"He said he needed the month's receipts to see how we were doing."

"Does he do that often? Is that part of the pattern?"

"No. I send a weekly report every Monday. Includes deposit history."

John made a note. "Okay, then. Let me run some checks on the players and see if anything comes up. One last question. Did you have duplicate keys made for the apartment?"

"No. I have both of them. One on my keyring, the other in my car."

"Smart woman," he grinned. "I don't know what's going on, Marlie, but I am good at my job. We'll figure it out." He put away his notebook, capped the pen and returned it to the cup. With a last smile he made for the front door. "I'll let you know if I find anything. Remember, I saw the carton first."

My turn to smile. I was happy as a clam at high tide. Someone else shared the load.

Chapter 17

Saturday morning, as a reward to myself, and a cowardly retreat, I packed a small bag, locked the now secure front door of my apartment and drove down to San Luis Obispo for the weekend.

I love the town, its quirky little shops and its excellent restaurants. I got a room at The Apple Farm on the edge of town, tossed in my bag and headed out. It felt good to be away, to be outside and stretch my legs. There's a lot of physical mileage in my history.

Always feels good to get out and move. Wandering the tree lined narrow streets relaxed my mind as well as my legs. I stopped for a sandwich, a cup of tea at another place, and bought a bag of salt water taffy.

Back at the inn I had a nice dinner and then retreated to my room. After a hot shower I curled up in the four poster bed with my Kindle, more relaxed than I had been in weeks.

That night I slept like an old dog on a sunny porch.

A basket of warm muffins was served to my room for breakfast in bed. With that start on the day I was on the road for home. The top down on the Mustang let the wind blow out the last of the cobwebs. I tuned in the oldies station and sang most of the way home, the wind blowing half the words back down my throat. Traffic was light, the sun was shining and I fell in love again with the area.

By afternoon I was home, as relaxed as warm butter and almost as toasted from the sun. My lips curled in a smile as I dropped down the last curve to Jade Beach, wondering why I didn't do this more often.

Until I turned into my street and saw the police cars.

Sunday is the quietest day of the week in Jade Beach. The cannery is closed, the deckhands are sleeping or hungover and a general calm pervades the salty air.

Not today.

I had to park across the street from the gates. My parking place was occupied by a Sheriff's cruiser, the handicap spot by a Monarch squad car. An ambulance was backed up to the open front door.

I jogged across the street towards the office where I ran into Paul. Literally. I was half a step inside at the same time he bolted out the door, slamming into me and knocking me backwards. I spun around, got my hands down to break my fall and caught my balance before I actually hit the ground.

"Watch out!" Paul yelled, staggering back from the impact. He called me a name before his eyes widened with recognition. Regaining his own balance he was in my face. "Where the hell have you been? You're fired! Get your stuff the hell off my property! Now!"

Spittle flew from his lips as he yelled, punching the air with a stiff finger pointed at me. I backed out of range just as a heavy hand clamped down on Paul's shoulder and he went down on one knee.

John Kincaid held him there and looked over at me. "You okay?"

I nodded.

John reversed his hold on Paul and helped him up.

"I'm gonna talk to my dad," Paul said, his face crimson, glaring at John. "Your job is in Monarch. Not here!"

"You're wrong, Paul," John said, dropping his hand. "This is part of my jurisdiction, too. Along with the Sheriff's department and Highway Patrol. You calmed down now?"

Paul shook himself like a wet dog. "I don't have to calm down. This is my property."

"Wrong again. This is a crime scene. Until it's released it's my property."

"You're gonna be looking for work, too," Paul threatened.

"I was looking when I came here. Now I want you off the property, Mr. Murphy. The facility is temporarily closed."

"You can't do that. My customers need to get to their stuff. You're inhibiting my business. I'll call my lawyer."

"You do that. You call from home. For right now, this is my crime scene and I need it cleared. I'll let you know when you can reopen. Until then it's off limits."

Paul's color deepened. I was afraid he was going to stroke out. Even the whites of his eyes had gone pink. He glared at John, his mouth hanging open. Without another word he turned around and left, shoving me out of the way with his shoulder as he passed.

I resisted the impulse to kick his butt.

"You sure you're okay?"

I turned back to John. "Yeah, I'm good. What's going on?"

184

"There was a break in," he said. "Where were you?"

"In San Luis."

"What time did you leave?" He glanced at his watch.

"Yesterday morning. I just got back. Was anything taken?"

John looked me in the eye, his face serious. "Do you know Steve Harris?"

I nodded. "Yeah, he's the weekend guy. He works here. Why?"

"He's dead, Marlie. He was killed."

My knees went weak. "He's dead?"

John nodded, watching my face. "I'm sorry, honey."

"What happened?"

He took my elbow and tugged me inside the office, guiding me to a chair in the waiting area.

Four other men occupied the office, all of them behind the counter.

One was taking pictures with a digital camera, one crouched before the recording unit, his head almost inside the cabinet.

Another was brushing the door knob to the back room with a small brush. The fourth was picking up scattered papers from the floor, sliding them back from a deep brown splotch on the carpet. Some of the papers were stained crimson or brown in spots and streaks.

The men worked quietly, their sounds mostly rustling or the squeak of shoe leather as they shifted position.

"You okay? You want some water?"

I shook my head. "No, I'm good. What happened?"

John squatted in front of me and dropped a hand on top of my folded ones. "Mr. Harris was shot. It looks like a robbery. Was there cash in the office?"

"We keep a hundred on hand to make change, mostly small bills. He might have taken a payment or rented a unit, I'd have to look at the daily log."

"No large amounts?"

"Not this time of the month, no. Around the first is the busiest. Even then, most of our payments are by check or credit card. We rarely have more than a couple of hundred in cash."

Another man interrupted and John excused himself. I stayed put but my eyes roamed the office. So familiar. So warm and welcoming. I had decorated it myself, from the carpet to the plants to the paintings on the walls. Even the rug behind the counter that was now a splotch of dark brown. Through the window I saw the ambulance leave. No siren, no lights.

John was back shortly. "Come on, let's step outside," he said, a hand on the back of my waist turning me towards the open front door.

When we were outside I took a deep breath and blew it out. "What happened, John?"

"Here, Marlie, sit down," he pointed at a bench.

I sat and he took a seat beside me, picking up my hand and holding it.

"Steve Harris is dead. He was shot."

Tears squirted into my eyes and I blinked. That nice old man. His only fault was talking too much. Because he was lonely. A single hot tear slid down my cheek.

"Was it a robbery?"

"You'll have to tell us. We don't know if anything is missing. From the looks of it Steve was either carrying a stack of paper or fell back into one. Those pages on the floor are blank."

"Maybe he was loading one of the printers or the fax machine. We keep reams of blank paper in that cupboard, the one with the door open."

"Is there a backup for the recorder? In another room?"

"No. There's only one. In the cabinet."

John shook his head. "It's smashed. The tape is gone. We'll canvas the customers, see if anyone heard anything."

"If they did I'm sure they would have reported it."

"No one has come forward yet."

Tears flooded both eyes. "Did he suffer?"

John squeezed my hand. "No. It was quick."

I sat there, my hand folded inside John's and sent up a prayer for Steve.

In a few minutes I freed my hand to wipe my eyes and my chin where tears dripped freely down the front of my shirt.

"Come on, let's get you upstairs. There's nothing for you to do now. We'll lock it up when they're through in there. A hazmat team will come clean up when forensics is done." He stood up and took my arm. "Come on, Marlie."

I let him guide me upstairs.

I put on a pot of coffee, my answer to every situation, and got down some mugs. When the coffee finished brewing I filled a couple of mugs and joined John in the living room.

He put away his notebook when I sat down and picked up his coffee. "Thanks, I needed this. I only had one cup this morning. My brain doesn't function till about the third one."

I nodded. "I know that feeling. When did you get here?"

"A little after eleven."

While I was lying in bed eating warm muffins Steve Harris was being murdered.

"Do you know when it happened?"

John set his mug on the coffee table. "Sometime this morning. I got the call and came right over." He gave me a dark look. "I thought it was you. Scared the hell out of me."

"Me? I wasn't even here."

"I know that now. The guy that called it in just said the manager was hurt."

"What could have happened? Steve couldn't offend anyone with a three week head start."

"How long have you known him?"

"I hired him. I didn't like the woman that was here so I let her go and hired Steve."

"Anyone have a problem with him? Ever complain?"

I shook my head. "Only about his talking."

"He talk a lot?"

"Always. I had to warn him a couple of times."

"About talking?"

"Yeah. He'd get bored in the office and lock it up to go out and visit with a customer. For a couple of hours at a time."

"That the only problem you had with him?"

"Pretty much."

"You sure? Marlie I need anything you've got right now. Were there other problems with him?"

"I got on him a couple of times for giving out too much information."

"In what way?"

"My dad had a heart attack last year and I took off to see him. Steve told everyone that came in, to explain why he was in the office. A dozen customers sent me sympathy cards."

"No harm done," he said. "Nothing else?"

"Just the talking. He was the loneliest man I've ever known. He didn't so much talk to you as at you. You know what I mean? He wanted an audience not a conversation. I think he talked to the plants."

"That's common with the elderly. Nothing else?"

"Not that I can think of. I had to warn him several times not to volunteer information unless he was asked. He'd start filling out a contract and the customer would ask if he was the owner and off he went, telling the history of the Murphy family from the time they got off the ark. If he didn't know the answer he made one up."

"He lied?"

I shrugged. "It wasn't a deliberate lie, you know? He wanted to have something to say, to keep it going. He didn't talk to people as much as he talked at them."

"So he made up things to say."

"I can't think of a one that would get him killed."

"What kind of stories did he make up? Can you remember them?"

I sighed and thought about it. "One I remember was him telling a customer my husband was killed in Afghanistan, a war hero."

"Harmless," John said.

"By itself, yes. The lady kept bringing me cookies and flowers 'for my loss'. I didn't 'lose' him – I divorced him."

"He was in Afghanistan?"

"The closest he ever got to sand was Pismo Beach."

"Why did Steve say he was a war hero?"

"He had no reason. He just wanted to talk, to keep talking. I swear that man would talk himself to death." I stopped, realizing what I had said.

"Any others you remember? Anything someone could find offensive?"

"I don't know, John. Most of his stories were harmless exaggerations. Who knows what he told people? I know once he told Randy he was in the 'newspaper' business. Turned out he was a paper boy."

"Randy another customer?"

"Mm-hmm."

"Did Steve have a favorite customer?"

"Only the slow ones."

John smiled and set the notebook down.

"Who called it in? Do you have a name?"

"I don't, no. The station will have it. Why? Is it important?"

"I have no idea. I wondered who it was, that's all."

"I can get it," John said.

"Probably doesn't matter. Just curious."

John checked his notebook, flipping pages, looking for something.

Suddenly there were shouts, loud voices. Someone was pounding up the stairs, then banging on the door.

John moved like a huge cat, edging me out of the way to get there first. His gun was in his hand by the time he cracked the door open to look outside.

Burke shoved hard, pushing John back a step and rushed to me.

"Are you all right?" He grabbed me and yanked me against his chest, his arms so tight I had difficulty catching my breath.

"Let go, Burke," I said, trying to get my arms between our bodies. "I can't breathe."

Finally wedging a hand between us and shoving against his chest, he loosened his hold. Sliding his hands up to my shoulders he held me and looked into my face.

John holstered his gun and took my elbow, tugging me away from Burke.

"Come on, Marlie, sit back down and drink your coffee." He guided me to the couch while Burke followed, running both hands through his hair. The blond locks stood on end. I saw his hands shaking when he brought them down.

"That's some entrance," John said, once I was seated. "What's all the uproar?"

Burke literally fell back into the chair like a deflated balloon. His head dropped to the back of the chair and he closed his eyes, taking in a deep breath.

"The call on the radio said the manager was shot and DOA. I thought it was Marlena."

A closer look showed him pale beneath his tan, like the tan had been badly sprayed on. As I watched the color came back much like one of my blushes.

Burke leaned forward and reached for my hand. "Are you okay?"

I was getting a little tired of that particular question.

"I'm fine. I wasn't here. It was Steve."

"The old man?"

I nodded.

Burke looked at John, who sat beside me holding his coffee cup. He might have come for tea from his demeanor as he watched Burke.

Burke shook himself and sat up. "That scared the crap out of me. You have any more coffee?"

"Kitchen," I said. "I'll get it."

"I will," John said, standing. "You sit and try to relax."

While John went into the kitchen Burke squeezed my hand between his. "Are you okay? Were you hurt?"

"I wasn't here," I said.

"Where were you?"

I looked at him. "Gone. What difference does it make? That kind, gentle man was killed. In the office. Minding his own business. He never hurt a soul in his life."

"Someone thought he did," Burke said, letting go of my hand to take the cup John held out.

"You think someone was after Steve?" John asked, sitting beside me again.

"Had to be that or money," Burke answered. "A robbery?"

John shook his head. "Marlie hasn't counted the money yet to see if any is missing. She doesn't think there was more than a couple of hundred on hand."

Burke scrubbed his face with the hand not holding the cup before taking a sip and setting the cup on the coffee table. I noticed his hand trembled.

He took in a load of air and blew it out. "What happened?"

John's turn to shake his head. "That's what we're trying to figure out. What brings you here?"

"I told you. The radio. Call said the manager was shot." He looked at me with warm, dark eyes. "I thought it was you. My heart tried to beat its way out of my chest all the way here."

"Where were you?" John asked. Was I the only one noticing the interrogation?

"On the freeway," Burke replied. "Coming back from Paso."

"You live in Paso?"

Burke shook his head again. "No, why?"

"Just wondered," John said. "Where do you live?"

"I get it," Burke said. "Okay, fair enough. I live in a motor home most of the time. It is currently parked out back in Space 29. I was in Paso for my niece's birthday party yesterday. I stayed over. I was coming home down the 101. Anything else?"

"No, that's good. You live in a motor home? No permanent residence?"

Burked sighed. "Am I a person of interest? Is there some reason for these questions? Why aren't you looking for the guy that did this?"

"Was it a guy?"

Burke picked up his cup with both hands and took a noisy drink. "I don't know what your problem is. I told you where I was. Where were you?"

John smiled at him. "I was home. I live in Monarch, just over the hill."

"Well, do you have any idea what happened?"

John nodded. "I know what happened. I just don't know why."

"You think maybe you could share?" Burke's voice sounded tight. A little muscle in his jaw jumped.

"Could," John said and sipped coffee.

"Damn it, man, what the hell happened?"

John smiled the coldest smile I'd seen on a human. Looked like one of those cartoon snakes in a Disney movie. "Someone," he said, stressing the word, "shot and killed Steve Harris in the office downstairs."

Burke snorted and sat back, closing his eyes. After a minute he opened them and looked at John. "Thanks, that's a big help."

"Welcome."

When nothing else was forthcoming Burke looked at me, again reaching for my hand. "Are you sure you're okay? Do you want to go to the hospital?"

I tugged my hand free and picked up my own mug. "I wasn't shot. I wasn't even here. I'm upset and I'm mad as hell but I'm all right."

The three of us sat there then, no one saying anything, each in his own thoughts. I finally broke the silence getting to my feet. "Anyone want more coffee?"

"I'll take a refill," John said.

"I'll take a beer," Burke said.

"No beer, Burke. I haven't been to the store. I have Diet Coke or juice?"

He shook his head. "That's all right. I need to get home anyway. Get cleaned up." He stood up and took his cup into the kitchen. When he came back he paused to give me a look. "How about dinner? Can I bring dinner by? You're not going to feel like cooking."

I never felt like cooking but something perverse took control. "No, thanks. I'm gonna fix something later. Thanks for coming by."

He stepped in front of me and gathered me for a gentler hug. "Of course, Marlie. If you change your mind, you have my number. If I can do anything, give me a call. I'll be in the back tonight."

I nodded. He kissed me on the cheek, stepped back and headed for the front door. "I'll report to Miller, I have to see him anyway. Keep me in the loop," he said to John. "I want to know what's going on. This one is personal."

"Will do, chief," John said and we watched Burke go out the front door.

When he was gone we sat in the quiet for a while before John, too, stood up to leave. I followed him to the door where he turned to face me. "It's going to be okay," he said softly. "We'll get whoever did this. You get some rest. If you need anything call me."

"Okay, and thanks. For everything."

"It's my job," he said, tipping my chin up to look into my eyes. "We'll get him, honey."

I smiled at him and locked up behind him. I gathered cups and took them to the kitchen. I was surprised to see it was almost dark. The fog was coming in, thick curtains of mist blowing down the street in visible clouds, pulling the chill air along with it. It was a fitting end to the day.

My mouth had that thick too much coffee taste and I sure wasn't hungry. I brushed my teeth and went to bed early, saying a prayer for Steve to find a listener in heaven.

Chapter 18

The office remained closed on Monday. Since I couldn't work I decided to go talk to Papa Murphy. He was normally at Kelly's in the mornings, holding court with the other old timers. I hoped to catch him there.

At Kelly's I remembered to grab a cup on the way in. I paused and looked around, spotting Papa in a large booth on the right, just in front of the plate glass windows. Paul sat next to him, Randy and another elder across from him. I made my way over and waited to be acknowledged.

"Agnes!" Mr. Murphy called every female, regardless of age, Agnes or Abigail. It saved him the embarrassment of forgetting a name and giving him time to figure it out. Sometimes he did it to show your ranking of importance to him.

"This is Abner and Randy," he said, introducing his companions.

"I know Randy," I said with a nod. "Good morning, Paul. It's nice to meet you Abner." I shook hands with Abner.

"These old geezers are leaving," Papa said with a tilt of his chin. Abner hurried to stand up while Randy took his time, sliding across the bench with his coffee cup.

"When you gonna open up?" He asked as he got to his feet.

"The lot's open now. Only the office is closed. I have to wait till the police give me the go ahead before I can open the office."

"Where am I gonna pay my rent? I don't want no late charge."

"I'm sure we'll be open before the first. Don't worry."

"All right then. No late charges."

"Not as long as you pay by the tenth," I repeated for him, the hundredth time. He was one of those who waited until five minutes to close on the tenth to pay his rent, hanging onto the money as long as possible. Who knows why? He had the money in his account. Several times he had called just before closing that he was on his way and I had waited for him, giving him an additional half hour so he wouldn't have to pay the late fee.

"Fair enough," he said and stood. "Sorry about the old guy."

I found that funny since Steve was five years younger than Randy and suppressed a grin. "Thank you, Randy. You have a nice day now."

"I can get to my shop?"

"Yes. The gates are working. It's just the office that's temporarily closed."

With a last nod he ambled over to the counter where Abner was perched next to an empty stool. He took the seat but kept his eyes on us. I was pretty sure he could hear from there, too. It's what made him such a good lookout at the facility.

"I assume from that, you know about the incident at the facility," I said when Randy was gone.

198

"I heard about it," Papa said, stirring sugar into his coffee. "Have you had breakfast?"

"I'm good, thank you."

Papa shook his head. "No you're not." He stuck a hand up. The waitress waved and he put his hand down. "You women. I bet you didn't eat last night and skipped breakfast. I always eat a good breakfast. Keeps me fit."

The waitress joined us, order pad in hand. "What can I get you, Papa?"

"I'm good, Sally. This young lady needs the Farmhand, with a peach muffin. How do you want your eggs?"

"Scrambled, please. And thank you."

The waitress called Sally looked at me for a long minute. "I'm sorry, dear. That must have been terrible for you. I'll get this right in. Coffee?"

"Please," I said and wondered how she knew. A look from Papa sent her on her way. "How does she know? Does everyone know?"

Paul nodded. "Small town," he said. "On top of that, Sally knows everything. She's like Google in sneakers. What can we do for you, Marlena?"

"I wanted to tell you how sorry I am," I said, looking at Papa.

"Why? Did you shoot him?"

I blinked. "No, sir. I didn't."

"Then no need for you to apologize. How are you holding up? Is there anything we can do for you?"

"No, sir. I wanted you to know I'm sorry it happened." Why was I here? They obviously knew what happened, probably had more information than I did.

Paul reached across the table to pat my hand where it rested beside my coffee. "We're sorry, Marlena. Sorry this happened. I can only imagine how bad you feel. I hope we're not going to lose you."

"Why would you lose me? This has nothing to do with me."

"Well, a single woman, living alone, over a murder scene. We would completely understand if you felt compelled to move."

"I hadn't even thought of it," I said, honestly.

"The police came by yesterday afternoon," Papa put in. "Do you have anything new? Anything this morning?"

"No, sir. There was a van there this morning, when I left. The closed signs are up although the front door was standing open. I left them to it."

"Smart girl," Paul said, a sincere look on his face. "We're gonna close the office this week, give you some time off. With pay, of course. We'll put a notice up so you don't have to do a thing. When the police are through with the office, we'll get it cleaned up."

"They took care of that," I said. "I haven't seen it but there was a hazmat truck there already. Detective Kincaid said they'd be thorough."

Paul shook his head. "Not enough. We'll get the carpet replaced, get the office painted. What color would you like? No pink, though. Too girly." He smiled at that.

"No need really. The carpet, yes. It was, well, ruined. That needs to be done. I was going to ask about that."

"Ordered it this morning. A sand color. That will go with whatever color you want to paint the walls. Go over to the hardware store in Monarch. Greg's. You know it?"

"Yes, sir, I've bought things there before."

"Pick out a couple of gallons of paint, whatever you like and put it on the account."

"Do you know how long the office is going to be closed?"

"Just a couple of days," Papa Murphy put in. "Here's Sally."

The waitress appeared at my side and put down a plate full of food – three strips of bacon, a slice of ham, and two sausage patties took up one side, scrambled eggs and home fries on the other. A separate small plate held a fat, golden muffin that smelled of ripe peaches.

"Can I get you anything else?" She asked. "That muffin is still warm, just out of the oven. New batch. You should eat it first, so it don't get cold."

"This is fine," I said, looking at the plate. "I don't think I can eat all this."

"Sure you can," she smiled. "The secret is one bite at a time. Try it," she winked and left us.

"I can't eat all this."

"Eat what you can," Papa said. He leaned forward and dropped his voice. "No matter what she says, take the muffin home for later. Nuke it for half a minute and it's just right. I do it all the time."

I smiled and reached for the salt.

"Will it bother you to talk while you eat?" Paul asked.

I shook my head and bit into a strip of bacon.

"Have they found anything?"

"Not that I know of," I answered.

"Well, not to sound crass or anything, but how much did we lose? You have any idea yet?"

I swallowed and took a sip of coffee. "Not a dime," I answered when my mouth was empty. "Saturday's rents were in the deposit bag in the back office, along with the payment log. It appears he had just opened the office when he was shot."

"Not a robbery then," Paul said. "How about petty cash? Did you check that?"

"I checked, Paul. It's all there. Not even a penny off."

"Do you think he pissed someone off?"

"Not enough to kill him. The only thing that man was ever guilty of was talking too much. You know? He loved to talk, didn't matter what subject, he just loved to talk. I think it was because he was lonely."

"How about family? I looked over his job application and didn't see any listed."

"He mentioned a brother in Texas but I have no idea what his name is. The police may know more about that. I'll ask them."

"Yeah good idea," Paul said. "You're pretty thick with Kincaid. He might tell you."

"I'm friends with John. I can ask."

"Doesn't matter," Papa said. "We can't compensate some guy in Texas. Immediate family only. Hold his paycheck in case someone contacts us. If it isn't claimed in a few months, toss it in a deposit."

Ouch. That was a cold decision and surprised me from Papa Murphy. I knew they didn't know Steve but still the man had died, been killed while working for them. My appetite left the building. I put down my fork.

"Well, thank you for breakfast," I said, wadding up my napkin. "I better get back over there."

"I told you to take the rest of the week off," Paul said. "I'll get an ad in the paper, find a replacement for the weekends. Till we do, close up on the weekend. You can't be working seven days a week. I have your home number and your cell number. If we need anything else, I'll give you a call." He patted my hand again. "This may sound terrible but we're very glad it wasn't you, Marlie."

"Thank you," I said, not sure what was the proper response for we're glad you didn't get shot to death. I felt the same way only I didn't think expressing it was appropriate. "Thanks for breakfast, too," I said and scooted out of the booth.

"One more thing," Papa Murphy said. "Take the muffin."

Chapter 19

On the way home I thought about the Murphy men and their attitude. While Steve technically worked for me he was still an employee of theirs. Paul made out his paycheck every two weeks just like he did mine. Their cavalier attitude to his death bothered me. I wondered if they would have been more concerned had it been me. Papa Murphy surprised me the most.

Pulling into my parking place I saw the van was still in front of the office. John Kincaid's silver pickup occupied the space next to it.

I went around to the open front door and stuck my head in. Two men in white coveralls sat at the counter while another stood beside John. Gritting my teeth I went in and glanced behind the counter. A huge square of carpet looked wet. The deep brown splotch was gone. I still shuddered.

"Marlena," John said with a smile. "What are you doing here?"

"To tell the truth, I don't know," I smiled back. "Habit, I guess. How's it going? Did you find anything new?"

John came to join me while the guy he had been talking to left through the front door. I moved out of his way as he went around me.

"Not so far. How're you doing?"

"Good, thanks. I went to breakfast with the Murphy's. Let them know what was going on."

"How did that go?"

"All right, I suppose."

John wrinkled his forehead. "What's wrong? They surely can't blame you for this."

"No, it's not that," I said, not sure what I was feeling and not ready to discuss it in committee.

"Anything new? Did they find anything?"

John waved an arm around the office. "It looks like someone opened the front door and shot him. You said none of the cash was missing. The computers, the video recorder, none of that was taken, just smashed up. It appears Steve was the target. Forensics might be able to get some video off the hard drive." He shrugged. "That's what we have right now."

"Have you found any family for Steve?"

"Not yet. I sent one of our officers to talk to his landlord. He might have more information if Steve filled out an application. Do you know any of his friends? Did he ever mention anyone he was close to?"

I shook my head. "Nope. You know he loved to talk. I've told you that. He never met a stranger. All the stories he told me were strictly him. You know, things he did, places he went, that kind of thing."

"Maybe Chuck will find something at his apartment."

"Chuck?"

"Sorry, Officer Chuck," he corrected. "We just call him Chuck. It's a habit."

"Chuck is his last name?"

John nodded. "Go ahead. Ask what his first name is."

I looked at him and saw he was trying not to smile. "Okay, what is Officer Chuck's first name?"

"Upton."

"Upton? Like Sinclair?"

"Uh –huh." The smile broke through. "Think about it, Marlie. Shorten it."

I got it and smiled. "Tough life growing up."

John nodded. "Yeah, that's why we just call him Chuck."

"And Chuck is the one going to Steve's apartment?"

"Yep. He's an excellent cop. He'll make detective soon. If there's anything there he'll find it."

"Are there other detectives?"

"In Monarch? Just me. I help out the Sheriff's department, too. I'm sort of a county detective stationed in Monarch. There's not enough crime in Monarch to justify a full time detective, so I work part time and get loaned out as needed."

"That's a good thing isn't it? Not much crime?"

"Yes, it is," he smiled. "There's enough to keep me busy without a lot of stress. I like it."

"I don't read the paper, or watch the local news so I have no idea what's going on. I guess I should."

"The paper only comes out once a week, on Thursday. There's not a lot of news in it, mostly ads and local happenings. For news, watch KSBY on television. They cover all the local stuff, anything of interest. Their truck was here earlier, covering this."

"I hate that," I said. "Not the kind of publicity we need."

206

"You may be surprised. There's also been several people looking for storage, or claiming to be looking. May just be curious, wanting to see the scene of the crime. Small town people are also very helpful people, not as callous as city people are. We still have barn raisings here."

"Barn raisings?"

"Yeah, like in old movies? A barn burns down and the whole town shows up to help put up a new one. Always ends with a barn dance," his eyes sparkled. "You must have seen one."

I nodded. "When I was a kid. Does anyone around here even have a barn?"

"As a matter of fact a friend of mine does have a barn."

"Whatever. I didn't think anyone on the coast had a barn."

"Look around sometime, out in the canyons."

"I'll do that the next time I'm out and about."

He took a step back. "I better get back to work. Is there something you needed? I get to talking and forget."

"No. Papa Murphy said to close the office the rest of the week. The gates will be open for customers to access their units, no new rentals. I don't have any vacancies right now so it's all right."

"Good. You can use a break. This can't be easy for you, having someone murdered where you live. And that brings me to the uncomfortable question I've been putting off."

I looked up at him. "What question? For me?"

"Yeah," he said and his smile faded. "Is there any reason someone would be after you?"

"Me? No. Not that I know of anyway. I don't think I've made anyone that mad. Not recently." I thought of Paul Murphy's scene at Kelly's and dismissed it.

"Any customers upset? Any lien sales of someone's stuff?"

"That goes with job. I haven't had a lien sale in ages, probably five or six months. As far as someone being upset? That's possible. I explain my rules to every person who rents a unit from me. I have them sign a paper that they understand those rules. And once a week someone will break one and when called on it, insist they never heard it before. Human nature."

"Recently? Anyone upset?"

"Probably. Enough to want to kill me? Don't think so. Sarcasm is a genetic defect in my family, along with a strange sense of humor. I've made people angry without meaning to. Again not recently."

"Had to ask," John said, with a sheepish grin.

"I understand. I'm surprised you hadn't asked earlier."

"Wanted to. Didn't want to lose my dinner partner."

My turn to smile. "I can't think of anyone I've made angry lately. I have no known enemies. I can't imagine Steve had any, either. I think you have a botched robbery attempt, although I don't know why they didn't take the petty cash. Maybe they were scared off before they got that far."

"It's a possibility. Among others."

"No hints?"

"Doing my job, ma'am," he said with a thick drawl. "I'll figure it out."

I nodded. "I bet you will, Detective Kincaid."

"I have another question," he said, his eyes serious. "Is there anything of a personal nature between you and Burke?"

"Not really. We're friends. I thought I had explained that."

"You did. I was double checking. He had an intense reaction when he thought it was you that was shot. Is it possible that he would like to have more of a relationship?"

"Burke is a born flirt," I smiled. "It's in his genes."

"He better keep it in his jeans," John smiled. "Or I may put it in his pocket."

I laughed in spite of myself. "Whoa there, Hopalong, slow down. No need for violence. I can handle him if need be. He's just being Burke."

"I'll take your word for it," John said adding his own smile. "For the record? I am interested. In more than dinner." He lifted my chin with one finger and dropped a soft kiss on my lips. "There's something to think about, take your mind off murder."

I left the office, smiling, and went around the corner headed for the stairs.

"That was a tender little scene," a voice said and I looked up at Patrick Murphy. "I'm gonna assume since you're kissing the cops you don't need any help."

My face flamed.

This time there was no smile from Patrick.

He looked royally pissed off, those blue eyes dark as storm clouds. "I have the paint for the office," he said in a chill voice. "Thought I'd save you the trouble. I'll take care of the painting. You seem to be busy."

With that he stepped around me and into the office. I noticed then he was carrying a can of paint in each hand.

It seemed to be my day for men.

Chapter 20

The previous night's fog hung around just off the harbor and by late afternoon began moving back in to reclaim the shore. I needed to eat, having skipped lunch, and nothing sounded good.

I finally made a peanut butter and jelly sandwich and poured a big glass of milk, taking them into the living room. I turned on the local news.

Beach Storage was the lead story. More great advertising.

The reporter, a lovely young lady who looked like she was too young to drive, stood in front of the office and did her report, covering just the basics without frill or fanfare. The last shot was of our sign as the voice over promised updates as soon as they were available.

I flipped the channels, looking for a movie, anything to take my mind off the murder. Nothing caught my attention so I turned off the television and sat in the silence watching the bread on my sandwich dry out.

Why would someone want to kill Steve? I couldn't get my head around it, the whole concept was beyond my understanding. Steve had been a tall, gentle giant with silver hair and a warm smile. He lived alone in a senior apartment building where the women outnumbered the men fifteen to one. He told me that the first weekend he worked. He believed he would have his pick of lovely gray-haired ladies who would want to spend their last years waiting on him hand and foot while preparing all his favorite foods. Didn't turn out that way. He told me that, too. I always thought he might find one that was deaf or hard of hearing and make a go of it. He deserved a lot better than being murdered at a part time job he took mostly to meet people. I hoped he hadn't met his murderer here.

~~~

I went over everything the next morning with John, using the back door to access the back office and avoiding the area behind the counter where Steve had died. The consensus of opinion seemed to be Steve was carrying a ream of paper when he was shot. The paper had flown like paper airplanes all over the immediate area. Some were blood stained – while others were not even creased. All were blank.

It was a customer that called 911.

He noticed the front door open, went in and found Steve. His call was recorded at 10:50, ten minutes before the office opened.

The front door should still have been locked.

Steve must have forgotten to lock it behind him when he came to work. His keys were still attached to his belt, including the new one for the front door.

I checked.

"Is there anything else you can think of?" John asked. We sat outside on the bench, sipping coffee.

"I've been over it and over it," I answered. "There is no reason to rob a storage facility. If a unit is broken into, nine times out of ten it's a friend, or relative, of the tenant. There have been cases where a couple of guys rent a truck, gain access and cut a bunch of locks at one time, emptying several units. And that's a gamble."

"Why so?"

"What if it's full of old clothes? Mattresses? There is no guarantee you'll find anything of value, even if you empty out four or five. You've paid for the truck rental and the gas and you still have to get rid of the stuff you steal. Unless you know what's inside why bother?"

"New world for me," John smiled. "Never thought about it."

"Take my word for it. Unless you happen to own a thrift store there's no profit in it."

"Do you have a theory? Now that you've had some time to think about it?"

"Me? No." I had thought about it, most of the night when I couldn't sleep. "Do you?"

He sighed. "There's a couple of ideas floating around. From what we know so far, it looks like someone opened the door and shot him. Then he or she took the disk from the recorder, busted up the equipment and left. Nothing is missing. Either someone wanted to get at Steve, or someone wanted to get at you and didn't know you were off weekends."

"Everyone here knows I'm off weekends," I said. "That eliminates the customer list."

"If they were after you, yes it does. You tell me Steve had no known enemies, was peaceful as a clam and liked everyone. What does that leave?"

I thought about it. "A random killing?"

John shook his head. "I don't think so. Not here in Jade. Maybe in LA or San Francisco, not here. It has to be related to this area if not to this storage facility. There are no other storage places around here?"

"Nope. This is it. Unless you want to drive to San Luis or Paso. The same question – why? There was the petty cash, the computers, the camera system and none of it was taken. Just busted up. No robbery."

"There is another possibility, you know."

I looked at him. "Someone after one of the Murphys?"

"It's possible," John nodded. "I've checked around on the sons. They both have reputations as playboys. Paul's been mentioned in more than one domestic report. The locals call Patrick 'Trick' for a reason. I hear he's broken every female heart in the county. Might have been an irate husband on the hunt."

"In the office?"

"It's a theory, Marlie."

"Are there others?"

John nodded. "Several. I think this is all related to those drugs being found here. Where did they come from? Were those the only ones? For that matter was that the first time? Maybe the wrong people picked them up. That could go fifty different ways."

"Wait a minute. Your theory is that my storage facility is a trading post for drug dealers? No way. Not going for that one. I'm far from stupid and I keep a close eye on this place."

"And this place wound up with nine cartons of high quality cocaine nicely packaged and left in an empty unit. And shortly after that a man seen near the unit with the drugs in it is found with a bullet in the back of his head on the side of the freeway. That has to be related. Someone took those cartons. Maybe it was the wrong someone."

"You guys let it get away," I defended. "You're the ones who put it back. Now you think another whole set of drug dealers found it and took it? That Steve was murdered over that?"

"If I've learned anything over the years it's nothing is impossible. Not when you deal with people. ."

My turn to sigh. "There's a connection, John. We just don't see it."

"We've been to this picnic before. I'll ask again. Do you think Burke is involved with the drugs?"

"I know he is. It's his job. I don't know what exactly he does, but he's been on this drug case for a long time, over a year. He told me that."

"I meant personally involved. Wouldn't be the first time someone undercover switch hit."

I thought about it. "I don't see it. I guess it's possible."

"He and the drugs showed up about the same time. That file you gave him? Never showed up. No one on the task force ever saw it. Not until I took in the one you gave me. So far he's the only one doing anything suspicious."

"Paul," I said, remembering him speaking Spanish on his cell phone. I told John about the incident.

"What was he saying?"

"No idea," I smiled. "Despite my looks, I'm only half Mexican. My dad insisted we speak English at home. The only Spanish I ever heard was from my grandmother when she visited."

John grinned. "Guess I'll cancel my Spanish class then."

I smiled back. "All I know for sure is he wasn't ordering food. I know those words."

"He may have picked up some Spanish. Common here in California."

I nodded. "I'm tossing out ideas." I remembered the harsh attitude of Papa and Paul. "What about Papa?"

"Irish Mafia? It's a stretch, Marlie. About the only thing the sons are guilty of is chasing women. The old man owns half of Monarch Beach, been here a long time. I don't think he'd take the risk. Lot to lose if caught."

"No worse than someone gunning for Steve. That's the biggest stretch of all."

One of the guys working in the office came out and interrupted, to tell John they were finished with the office and would be leaving shortly. I thanked him and we sat on the bench and watched them leave.

When they were gone, John looked at me with concern, his brows pulled down. "Are you going back to work in there?"

"Not today. Papa Murphy told me to take the rest of the week off. Paul is going to find a replacement for Steve, someone to work weekends. Patrick said he'd paint the office, do some stuff around here. I won't be going back till Monday."

"Can they do that? Just close up?"

"They can do anything they want. They own it. Besides, it's the slow time of month. The current customers can still get in, the gates are working. I'll change the recording on the phone for a few days, we should be okay till I get back on Monday. Emergency numbers on the front are Papa and Paul, and I'll be around most of the time."

"It's nice of them to redo the office," John said. "The carpet was the only real loss." He stopped and glanced at me. "Didn't mean to sound crude there."

"I know."

"Come on, enough of this. If you don't have to work let's go get something to eat." He stood and dusted off the seat of his pants. "Kelly's has ham steak tonight with fried sweet potatoes and greens. One of my favorites. We'll both feel better if we get something to eat."

"Sounds good to me."

"Come on, then. Lock up the office and you can ride with me. I'll bring you home."

John was right about the dinner at Kelly's – it was excellent and led to discussions of past Thanksgiving meals with family. I shared memories of making tamales on Christmas Eve with my dad and the weaving of palm fronds into little boxes, to cook rice dumplings called tipat, with my mom.

"I like rice," John said. "That sounds good."

"Sorry, John. I gave up my frond weaving when I left home. My folks are both great cooks. I tend towards finger foods, like tacos and pizza."

He chuckled. "At my place it's anything that can be stuffed between two pieces of bread and hit with mustard. Nothing fancy about it. Also why I eat here a lot." He motioned around us at the other diners. "My home away from home."

"I'll remember," I said.

"Hey, dinner on me any time I'm here."

"I'll remember that, too," I said. "This was a nice break. Thank you."

"Welcome."

Chapter 21

The next day I had the apartment clean, the sheets changed and the laundry done before noon. What was I going to do for the next four days? I was suddenly aware of how shallow my life had become. Work, home, work, home. No wonder I had accepted Burke's company so readily. Was he a friend or a welcome break in a boring routine?

I made a peanut butter sandwich for lunch, took three bites and tossed it. My snug and comfortable apartment was like a beige and crimson cell with house plants. I locked up and went downstairs.

Signs on the front door and beside the gate notified customers of the temporary closure to the office. The front door stood open right next to the sign saying it was closed.

I went inside. Paint fumes greeted me. The counters were gone and so were the cabinets. Drop clothes covered the floor of the empty room. It looked a lot bigger without furniture. Watching my step I went back to the kitchen where I heard noises.

The office counters, the chairs and most of the missing office furniture was stacked and piled along the walls, leaving a narrow passage to the sink. Patrick Murphy rattled the carafe for the coffee pot under the faucet.

"You want me to do that?" I asked from the doorway.

Patrick started and spun around. "What are you doing here?"

I eased my way along the passage to his side and hip checked him to the side. "I'll get this," I said. "It's tricky if you don't jiggle the on button." I put the water in the pot, added the basket of fresh grounds and pushed the on button five times. On, off, on, off and on. For some reason it was the only way it worked. I intended to buy a new one eventually.

Steve only drank tea and he used the microwave so there had been no rush.

"That a secret code?"

I glanced at Patrick who had moved back against a stack of boxes. "She's a girl coffee pot. Temperamental."

"I'll remember that."

"It's something in the switch. For future reference it's five clicks and it works fine." I pulled a couple of mugs from the cupboard above the sink. The smell of fresh coffee swelled around us. "You want sugar? Cream?"

"Blond," he replied.

I got down the Coffee Mate and pulled a spoon from the drawer.

"You didn't tell me what you're doing here."

"Habit. Bored. Curious. Pick one."

Patrick's lips curved up in a smile, his eyes warm and bright. "I'd bet it's all three."

"You might be right," I said. The coffee pot gurgled, hissed and sighed to a finale. I poured two cups of coffee, added creamer to mine, and slid one towards Patrick.

We had to shift a little to make room for raised elbows and cups in the small space.

"You need any help with this?" I indicated the stacks around us. "The painting? Anything I can do to help?"

Patrick blew on his coffee and took a sip. "I got it but thanks. That's nice of you."

"It's my office."

"I'm sorry about the other guy. Were you close?"

"No, not really. I spent a few days training him, saw him a few times on the weekend, when I was going in or out."

Patrick nodded and sipped more coffee. "Smart. Getting close to an employee can be trouble."

"You had that problem?"

I don't know why I said it. It just popped out.

The warmth in his face, the slight smile died. "Which story did you hear? The one about the gal that tried to kill herself? Blamed me for breaking her heart? Or the one about the gal that smashed in my wind shield down at the pier?"

"I didn't mean anything, Patrick. I just asked. Making conversation."

He gave me a long, cool look. "You're not blushing. You getting used to me?"

"I hope so."

"Me, too," he said and the way he said it, the look in his eyes, I felt the heat climb up my neck and fill my cheeks, right to the tips of my ears.

Patrick laughed, a belly laugh, filling the small space we shared. He laughed so hard his hand shook and he spilled coffee down his shirt front.

That sobered him up although those blue eyes again sparkled. "Now look what you made me do," he said, smiling.

"You deserved it. You're lucky I didn't pour mine on you."

"You would, too. You're the type."

"What type is that, Patrick?"

The space between us changed, became charged and heavy. Patrick's eyes darkened even as I looked into them.

I had nowhere to go, pressed against the kitchen counter with his body blocking the narrow passage, between furniture and stacked boxes.

He set his cup atop the stack at his side, holding me with his eyes. He reached for me, his arms sliding around my shoulders, and tugged me closer if that was possible.

We were almost touching when all hell broke loose.

The floor lifted and dropped and lifted again before rolling sideways. A low rumble filled the room, pressing against my ears. Boxes groaned, swayed and began to fall around us.

Patrick yanked me against his chest and shoved my head into his shoulder, his head coming down on mine. He lifted one hand to cover my head and shoved me against the tower of boxes while the floor shook and heaved.

Earthquake!

With my head jammed against Patrick's chest I couldn't see a thing. I could hear boxes falling, dishes rattling in the cupboards. Car alarms sounded from outside, something out there crashed with a roar.

The floor shook again, side to side.

I clutched Patrick, my arms around his waist.

The building continued to move. Up, down and sideways, the walls groaning. Glass popped and tinkled somewhere close.

I squeezed my eyes closed.

For over a minute we huddled together, our arms tight around each other.

There is a dull roar beneath every earthquake. Any Californian can tell you about it.

Then it's over.

Patrick held me against his chest another minute before he raised his head and looked around.

I slowly lifted my head and released my grip on him.

The boxes had shifted and fallen into the narrow access space. They looked like a derailed train now, some tilted, some end on end. Two had fallen on the counter, one knocking the coffee carafe off the burner and into the sink, now littered with shards of broken glass.

Patrick's breath was warm on my face. "Are you okay?"

I took a breath. Nothing hurt. "Yeah, I'm good."

"That was a big one," he said.

Somewhere outside I could hear the car alarms going off. Things were still falling somewhere around us. I could hear the thuds and thumps.

"Stay right there a minute," Patrick said, pushing me against the only stack of boxes still in place. "Let me see if I can get us out of here."

With that he tried to turn around which meant me sucking in my belly and pressing hard against the counter while his body rubbed across mine.

With a little maneuvering he faced the opposite way, giving me his broad back. I watched the muscles in his back bunch and relax as he shoved and lifted cartons to the top of the pile. Others he literally tossed up and out of the way, over the stacks around us.

It took a while for him to get the path cleared.

A few times he passed me a box and I put it behind us so we could keep going forward. We finally reached the short hallway which was intact, and empty. We paused.

"You sure you're okay?" He asked when we cleared the kitchen.

"Yeah, but I wish someone would shut off that alarm."

He fumbled in his pocket, pulled out a key ring and pressed a fob. The alarm went silent. "Must have been my truck."

"Glad it wasn't mine," I said, with a shaky smile. "My keys are upstairs."

"Come on, let's see if we still have stairs." He took my hand and led the way through the office.

It was easy to see the crack that ran across the ceiling and down both walls. A bright strip of sunlight gleamed through the ceiling.

The drop cloths on the floor were covered in dust and pieces of plaster, some on them as big as pie plates.

"Watch your step," he said still leading the way. The front door was still open although the framing was higher on one side than the other. The front wall looked solid without cracks.

A whole section of the roof had fallen forward missing his truck by a foot. Coated in dust and plaster it stood where he had parked it.

My Mustang had not fared so well – the entire hood was beneath the roof, the wind shield shattered. Dust still floated in the air above it. Roof tiles covered the back seat.

Patrick helped me through the debris till we got clear of the damage.

Around us the asphalt had split in places and buckled in others. One long crack ran across the driveway, one side of it six inches higher than the other. A geyser of water shot ten feet in the air and splashed down into the crack.

Patrick went along the side of the office. "Where's the shut off?"

"Somewhere there. It was between the windows."

The windows were there, the glass wasn't. Shards glittered in the flower bed beneath the empty frames. The night blooming jasmine had fallen away from the wall and lay in the flower bed, the broken trellis weighing it down.

"Can't find it," he said, straightening up and carefully stepping back to where I stood. "Where's the main?"

"Street," I said and pointed.

With a nod he made his way across the uneven ground of the parking lot. I saw him kneel and shortly the fountain of water dwindled and died. He stood up again and wiped his hands along his thighs.

I looked at the stairs to my apartment. An advantage to that covered space where the two halves of the building joined– they appeared undamaged. I started for them and Patrick called out. "Leave it for now. Don't know how sound they are. We'll check later. We have to check the lot. Was anyone inside?"

"I don't know," I said, joining him. Several more cracks broke the asphalt, none of them as deep as the one in front.

One side of the gate had fallen flat while the other stood on its track.

Patrick looked at me. "You have a cell phone?"

I nodded and patted my pocket.

"Come on, let's see if anyone is hurt."

"Should I call 911?"

Patrick chuckled. "You and every other person in Jade."

I felt my skin flush.

Of course we weren't the only ones with damage. I looked at the garage and saw one side of the door had let go while the other side still held. There was a gap between the heavy door and its frame.

Patrick caught my hand and tugged. "Come on, Marlena, there may be someone stuck out there. Or hurt."

When we were through the gate we stopped and looked around.

Buildings One, Two and Four looked okay from where we stood, no visible damage we could see.

The asphalt was buckled in places, a few cracks running down the driveways.

Some of the doors on the units had popped completely free and lay in front of the gap they had previously covered. Other doors hung by a single hinge, blocked by boxes that had thrown their contents out into the aisle.

The entire front wall of Building Three had fallen straight out, like it was sliced off with a giant knife. The whole end of that building now exposed was the one occupied by Mrs. Murphy. The roof had dropped on to those rows of cartons we had just stacked there. The cartons held the roof off the ground. The ones on the bottom were squashed down, the sides bowed out. Bending I could see the paths between the rows looked like little tunnels. Roof tiles, pieces of wood and chunks of pink insulation fanned out from the foundation.

"How's it look over there?" Patrick called from the far corner where he had made his way to Building Eight. "Seven looks okay, but Eight has damage. Cracks all along the wall. Some of the doors are down."

"Three is a loss," I called back. "Whole end of it is down. The others look okay."

We were yelling back and forth when an aftershock hit. I sat down, right where I was, Indian style, crossed my ankles and dropped down on my butt. A grumble filled the air, the ground shook and lifted again.

Then it was silent.

"You okay?"

I got to my feet and waved to Patrick who was making his way to where I stood. "I'm good," I called and waited for him to join me. "This is bad," I said when he reached me.

"It is that," he agreed, looking around. "Gonna take more than a couple of tarps to cover this. We'll have to get a building inspector down here before we let anyone in. Don't want someone to get killed."

"Insurance?" I asked.

He nodded. "Not sure it's gonna cover this. Act of God clause, like flooding." He turned and pointed to the row of vehicles that appeared unscathed. "At least the vehicles and boats survived. I don't see any damage to them. Good thing they're out here in the clear."

"The owners can get them out," I said. "We can throw some plywood over that bad crack by the gate."

"To go where? This was a big one. We're not the only ones to suffer damage. Owners may just want to leave them."

I looked at Space 29. "Looks like your motor home is okay. So is Burke's. That boat trailer has flat tires, otherwise looks good." We wandered along the row and found no damage to the outside storage other than a couple of flat tires.

I pointed to the end of Building Three. "That's the biggest damage, your mom's big unit, the one without the walls."

Patrick laughed. "Good. Maybe she'll get rid of all that stuff."

We turned and made our way back towards the exposed end of the building. Carefully climbing around the fallen wall we got close enough to see the tunnels between rows of cartons and boxes that held the roof off the ground.

"We can't take the cartons out," Patrick said, bending to look under the roof. He went to one knee.

228

"Those cartons are supporting the roof. If we try to move them out, it's gonna fall. Need someone to check it out, see if we can jack it up. I told her fifty times to let me put those walls up in this unit. Might not have fallen if they were there for support." He got to his feet and dusted his hands against his legs.

"There is one bright spot," he said. "I hadn't started painting yet."

I laughed in spite of myself and he joined in.

"All right, let's go see those stairs," he said.

"Yes, please. I have to get home. I have nowhere else to go and my car is under the roof of the office."

Patrick stopped and looked at me. "Hang on a second. Stay right there."

He turned and jogged back to his motor home and disappeared around the side. I waited, looking at the collapsed end of Building Three.

The ground heaved again, up and down, another aftershock. I crossed my ankles and sat. Temblers were common after a quake. Sometimes the aftershocks last for days.

I stood up again and watched Patrick jog back to me.

He was smiling. "Motor home is good," he said. "Didn't even spill the salt."

I returned his smile. "Good for you!"

"No, good for you. You have a place to stay till we get the apartment checked out."

"I can't do that," I said. "I'm sure everything is all right upstairs."

"You are not going up those stairs till someone checks them out. The way the office cracked and fell, no way. You can stay in the motor home." He pulled out his keys and twisted one off. "Here you go. Batteries are all charged, the water tank is full so you're good for a few days. Should even be some canned food in the galley."

I tucked the key in the watch pocket of my jeans with no intention of staying in his motor home.

He went to the corner of the collapsed roof and dropped again to one knee. He caught the edge of the gutter and gave it a shake. The roof groaned. A small cloud of dust rose up.

"Pat! Get away from it," I yelled. "I can't pull that off you."

He stood and dusted his hands together, still looking.

I went to him and tugged on his arm. "Come on, man. Another shock could bring it all the way out here." I caught the back of his jeans and pulled. "Get back."

To my relief he backed up beside me.

"I think we can get some jacks under here and raise it. Get her stuff out," he said.

"I thought you wanted her to get rid of it."

He turned and grinned at me. "I do. And she knows it. Have to make every effort before I call in the heavy equipment and have it scraped to the ground." He was smiling, his eyes bright. "Dump that whole mess into a dumpster and call it done. All right, we've seen enough. Let's check the rest of the place." He led the way to the back of the property.

While there were cracks in the buildings, none had sustained the damages of Building Three. It was possible interior walls had sustained damage but for the moment it wasn't apparent. People's belongings were another matter. How they had stacked and stored would be the key to how well their things survived. No one had been in the lot at the time. That was a blessing. Had someone been inside at the time, they could have been killed.

Patrick and I walked the perimeter, staying in the middle of the aisle, not getting close to either side, just to be safe. He rattled a few doors and kicked at a corner to assure himself it wasn't going to cave in with the next aftershock.

It took us hours to check it all. During that time we heard numerous sirens flare and go in different directions. There were sudden, loud crashes somewhere nearby.

When we returned to the office, two customers waited at the broken gate. They looked like those dead eyed people you see on the evening news following a disaster.

Patrick left them to me while he went to the foot of the stairs.

The customers and I huddled in the early evening chill like refugees, exchanging stories. After I assured them several times that they couldn't get back to their units they left together, on foot.

The street had a foot deep crack down the center with one side was at least a foot higher than the other. At the very end of the street another geyser of water shot high in the air.

When they left I went around the corner to find Patrick. He was leaning against the back fender of my Mustang.

The entire front of the car was flattened including both front tires. The back half didn't look bad, the trunk undamaged.

Patrick heard me coming. "Sorry, Marlena, this is totaled. Hope you have good insurance."

"I do," I said. "Unless this is going to another one of those Act of God things. I hope it's covered."

"It will be a while before you know. The phone lines may be down. There's no cell service. Those stairs aren't safe. I got up the first few and then they got bouncy, like walking on a trampoline. You're not going to be able to get up there till I get them checked by the building inspector."

The tears fell then, hot streaks down my cheeks.

Patrick came to me and wrapped me in a warm hug. He made little pats on my back and murmured those senseless things we all do to someone hurt. I leaned on him for a little bit and let him comfort me. Then my father's blood coursed through my veins and I stood straight.

"Your truck seems to be okay. Go see if you can help someone else. I'll watch the gates."

"Call your cop buddy. See if he can come over."

"He's probably buried in calls. Go. I'll be fine."

Patrick looked at me. "All right," he said finally. "I'll check back later."

"Whatever. Go."

"I'm going to go check on my folks. I want you to promise me you won't try those stairs. They are dangerous. There's nothing up there worth dying for. Got it?"

"Yes, sir."

232

"Your word," he said. "Promise?"

"Promise."

"Use the motor home. Another shake and the whole place may come down. You're safe there. It's clear of buildings, nothing is going to fall on it."

I nodded.

"I mean it, Marlena. I'm going to hold you to that promise."

I nodded again. "Go."

With a last look he turned around and unlocked his truck. I watched him leave, the big truck bouncing over the cracks and ruts.

When he was out of sight I took another turn around the lot, watching my step. The last thing I needed was to turn an ankle or bust my butt in a fall.

I went back in the office and scrounged around for some paper which reminded me of Steve. One of the cabinets stacked in the kitchen yielded a ream of paper and in the drawer I found tape and a black marker. I printed a couple of closed signs by hand and took them outside. I taped them to the front door and the half of the gate still standing, knowing at the time it was a useless gesture but needing to do something.

The sun was sinking behind the eucalyptus trees at the end of the street. Someone had turned off the water that had been shooting into the air. Everything was quiet. No birds sang, no horns honked, no one's stereo blasted the air.

There was nothing to do and sadly, no home to go to. I toyed with the idea of trying the stairs but I had given my word and in my family that mattered. Rubbing my arms I headed for the motor home.

Chapter 22

I'd never been in a motor home. It really was a home on wheels. All the amenities of an apartment. The rear compartment held a full size bed, night stands, a television and DVD player.

The compact bathroom had a shower, the kitchen area had both a four burner stove and a microwave. A small table flanked by bench seats made a dining area and a short couch faced an end table and chair.

Poking around in drawers I found dishes, silver ware, even a coffee pot. The cupboard above held a can of ground coffee as well as a jar of decaf Taster's Choice, Coffee Mate and sugar packets. I filled the coffee pot with water and coffee and set it on a burner. In minutes the rich smell of coffee filled the air. I found a mug and poured myself some coffee.

Taking a seat at the table I relaxed for the first time in hours. I took the time to enjoy the coffee before I got back up and started looking through the cupboards I hadn't investigated.

One on the bottom was a treasure trove of canned goods. I had my choice now of soups, spaghetti, veggies or tuna. There were crackers and a jar of cheese, cans of peaches and pears.

I looked in the little fridge and found bottled water, a small jar of mayo and another of mustard.

Below that was a cupboard with two sauce pans and a skillet. Other dishes were in drawers.

With some milk and bread, I could live quite well in here I decided.

After a dinner of soup and crackers I made another pot of coffee and turned on the television in the front compartment. There were only three stations on, all local, but they were covering the earthquake, switching from location to location with video of each one.

I watched for a few minutes, long enough to learn three people had been killed in the quake and that I didn't know them. The epicenter was north of us, closer to San Francisco. When they switched to cover that city, I turned off the set.

It was full dark by then. Once the television was turned off I sat in darkness. The compactness of the unit made it easy to navigate. With a few steps I rinsed the coffee pot, my cup, bowl and spoon and set them in the sink. Another couple of steps and I was in the bedroom at the back.

I switched on the bedside lamp which shed a soft yellow glow. Another television was mounted on the wall facing the bed, the shelves below held DVD's contained by a bar across the shelf.

Even better, the drawers below held Patrick's tee shirts and sweats. I washed my face in the bathroom, careful not to use too much water. In the bedroom I peeled off my jeans and shirt and pulled on one of Patrick's tee shirts. It fell to mid-thigh and made a perfect night gown.

Hanging the towel on a hook I went to the back, opened one of the screened windows, turned down the bed and slid between clean, crisp sheets. Another aftershock shook the motor home. It rocked sideways a couple of times and settled. The last thing I remembered was thinking I'll never get to sleep.

~~~

Waking the next morning it took me a couple of seconds to realize where I was. I had slept hard. I got out of the bed, stretched and headed for the little bathroom. I used the facilities, washed my face again and looked through the little medicine chest above the sink. All the cupboard doors were fastened with latches to keep them from popping open. The medicine chest was the same – a metal clip that snapped to the side.

Inside I found bandages, aspirin, tooth paste, deodorant and all manner of miniature items. The most impressive was the folding toothbrush, still in a cellophane wrapper. I felt better just looking at it.

I loaded the coffee pot and while it gurgled along I went back to the bedroom. My clothes were on the foot of the bed where I had folded them the night before. There is no way I am going to wear the same panties another day so I pulled on my jeans commando and picked up my bra. I'm okay with double days there. I snapped it in place before looking in the drawer that held the tee shirts. I took the one on top and pulled it over my head. It was still long so I gathered the hem and tied a knot at the side. Maybe not stylish but it looked better than hanging almost to my knees. Checking the other drawers I found clean jeans which were never going to work, even if I cut off the legs. Closing that drawer I opened the top and found the treasure – clean socks. Tube socks. One size fits all. I smiled as I pulled those on and slipped into my sneakers. Good to go.

The coffee was ready by the time I was dressed so I rolled my panties into the tee shirt I had slept in and set them by the door. I would wash and return his shirt as soon as I got upstairs to my apartment.

After a breakfast of granola bars and coffee I washed the coffee pot and the few dishes I had used and set them to drain while I made the bed. It was almost eight when I stepped down from the motor home to look around.

The damage was still there.

The roof of Building Three was still down, the debris from its fall spread in a fan in front of it. The silence was noticeable – still no birds. In the distance I heard the faint whoop of a siren.

I walked as far as Three and stooped to see inside, wondering if there was a way to seal it so Mrs. Murphy's belongings wouldn't be open to the elements. If there was a way it wasn't apparent so I stood up and headed for the gate. I was half way there when Paul and Papa Murphy walked back and met me.

"How bad is it?" The first thing Paul said.

"Good morning," I said to Mr. Murphy. "How are you?"

Mr. Murphy smiled and nodded at me. "Good, good, my dear. And you? You look good," he said, his eyes drifting down.

"How bad is the damage," Paul said again. "We've got an inspector coming as soon as possible."

"Building Three is the worst," I said. "The whole end of the building is down, the roof fell forward. Building Eight has some big cracks and so do the driveways. The rest looks repairable. I haven't been in the apartment yet. Patrick said the stairs needed to be checked before I went up."

"I'm glad you're all right, Agnes," Mr. Murphy said with a pat on my shoulder. "We can't afford to lose you."

Paul had continued on down the drive, head turning as he scanned the lot.

"Thank you, Papa Murphy. How about you? Your home okay?"

"It's fine. Thanks for asking. Paul was the architect for the big house, you know." He always referred to his home as the Big House. "Doesn't even have a crack. Colleen lost a few of her knickknacks." He winked at me. "I don't count that as a loss."

We had made our way down to Building Three while we chatted. Paul stood, hands on hips, looking at the debris.

"What do you think?" Papa called as we joined him.

"I think if mom had let Trick finish the damn walls it would be fine. The way it is, I don't know. We'll have the inspector start here, see how bad it is."

"Patrick thought you might be able to jack it up, get Mrs. M's belongings out," I said.

"Trick is here?" Paul looked annoyed.

"Not now," I said. "This was yesterday. He was here when the quake hit, working in the office."

238

Paul snorted. "He's no expert, believe me. I'll talk to inspectors, Dad, get us some idea of how stable it is. Like I said, we'll start here first."

"No offense," I said. "I'd like to have the stairs checked. I need to get home. I can't do anything about my car without the insurance papers and they're all upstairs."

"You don't pay rent," Paul said. "We need to get these buildings fixed. People will start moving out. We can't afford that. No offense Marlena. I can bring in a motor home for you for a few weeks. "

"I'm sorry about your car," Mr. Murphy said, with another pat. "I'll have Paulie bring down the Porsche. You can use that till you get yours squared away. Get a room at that motel up on the freeway. We'll pay for that. You can stay there till we get your stairs fixed."

Mr. Murphy owned a Porsche convertible, a Rolls and an older BMW. The Porsche was his baby, a forest green gem he rarely drove. I know. It was stored in Building Eight when he didn't have it at home.

"That's nice of you, Papa. I think I can get a rental till mine is replaced. I just have to get to my apartment."

"That will be our priority, too," Papa said, cutting off Paul's objection. "In the meantime anything you need, anything at all, just let Paulie know. He'll have your stairs inspected."

Paul made a noise in his throat. "I'll get it checked, but don't hold your breath. It's going to be at least a couple of days before you can get up there. Call the motel, get yourself a room. You can get some clothes at Marine Supply to hold you over. Tell them to bill me."

"I'll look into it," I said, not wanting to mention the motor home.

Paul gathered some blocks of insulation and started tossing them against the fence where Burke had raked up some dead grass, fast food bags and loose bits of cardboard. I bent and gathered some pieces of broken wood and tossed them on the pile.

"Might as well wait for the inspector," Burke called, striding down the drive to join us. "Then we can bring in a skip loader and clear it. Haul it all off at once."

Burke shook hands with both men and nodded to me. He looked around, bent to look under the fallen roof. "You might be able to jack this up, get the stuff out," he said, straightening up. "If jacks won't hold it, cut a hole right here," he gestured at the arc of the roof. "Get the stuff out, cut it clear and reframe it, rebuild the end. Won't take too long."

"Paulie is the architect," Mr. Murphy said. "That will be up to him. There's nothing we can do now. I'll call and get the gate guys down here, get that gate fixed so the place is secure. Come on, Paulie."

"All right, Dad." Paul started up the drive way.

Mr. Murphy patted my shoulder one more time. "Paulie will bring the Porsche for you."

"No need, Mr. Murphy. I thank you for the offer. I'll get a rental car. It's going to be a while before they settle my claim. I'm sure they're going to be busy. How about the harbor? Much damage there?" I changed the subject to get away from the Porsche.

Papa made a patting gesture. "No major damage. A few boats took on some water. The Gem is fine, not even a crack," he said, talking about the bar and pizzeria he owned in next door Monarch Beach.

"That's good to hear. I'm glad it wasn't worse."

He scuffed his boots on the asphalt and stuffed his hands in his pockets. "Well, then, we'll leave you to it. Don't worry about cleaning up around here. We'll hire some men to do it. I told you to take the time off. Now you be a good girl and have a vacation. Do you need money?" He pulled one hand from his pocket and reached for his wallet.

"No sir, I'm good. What I really need is to get upstairs. Everything I have is up there – my clothes, my insurance papers, even my food! There has to be a way to get up there! The stairs don't look that bad."

Papa Murphy patted the air again with both hands and backed up a couple of steps. "Now, don't be anxious, dear. We'll see to everything. Paulie will bring the Porsche. You get a room at the motel, we'll cover your expenses. Nothing to worry about."

I bit my tongue to keep from screaming at this sweet old man. I didn't want the freaking Porsche. With my luck, I'd hit a tree or something before I drove it a block. There was no need for a motel room since I was staying in the motor home.

I sucked in a double lung full of air and blew it out slowly. "Thanks, Papa. It's not necessary. I'm going to need a rental car any way, until the insurance settles. That make take a while."

Mr. Murphy nodded once and held up a finger. "The thing is, Marlena, there are no rental car agencies here. You'll have to go to San Luis or over to Paso."

I felt my cheeks warm up as the flush crawled up my neck again. He was right. We were also short on taxis.

"Maybe you can give me a ride to San Luis."

"I can do that," Burke said, and joined us. "I heard you. I have to go to San Luis tomorrow morning. Will that do? I've got a meeting right now, just came by to see if you were all right, see how the place was. I'm late now," he said, looking at his watch.

I looked around at the lowering sun, the long shadows and realized the day was ending. I didn't want to leave the facility at all, and certainly not at night. With another sigh I said, "Tomorrow is fine, Burke. Thank you."

"Nine?"

"That's great. I'll be ready." In the same clothes, again. At least Patrick had a drawer full of clean socks. And tee shirts.

Chapter 23

The guys all left and once they were gone I went back to the motor home. Nothing I could do now anyway, except open a can of soup and settle in for the night. Even my Kindle was upstairs. I thought but did not vocalize a few choice phrases.

I unlocked the motor home, climbed in and looked through the cupboards again while a fresh pot of coffee perked. I was going to need a list of things to replace when I finally got home. Nothing looked good so I used the same cup I had washed this morning and poured myself some coffee. Things are always better with coffee.

A loud bang echoed through the air, followed by a metallic rattle. Afraid someone just ran into the gate I took off for the front at a run. Rounding the curve I collided with Patrick Murphy. Literally. He dropped a plastic bag he was carrying and caught my arms, steadying me for a minute before he set me back.

"I'm sorry," I said immediately. "I heard a noise, sounded like someone hit the gate."

He bent and picked up the bag and thrust it at me. I caught it by reflex, clutching it to my chest. Whatever was inside was soft.

"It was me at the gate. I got the other half up and it's working. You won't have to worry about anyone prowling around in the lot tonight."

"Wow, good job, man. The computer's working?"

He nodded. "It's up and running, the gates are back on automatic. Let's keep it closed till we get it cleaned up back here, have it inspected."

I smiled. "Thank you. That's a relief. I didn't want to stand out there all weekend."

"Hang on a second," he said, and went back toward the gate. Another metallic rattle sounded as the gate slid back as usual. I watched Patrick go through, pick something up and push in a code to come back through the gates. He had an extension ladder balanced on his shoulder. With a toss of his head he motioned me to follow him. We went down the drive to where the end of Building Three lay almost flat, balanced on the boxes and cartons. Bending at the waist he shoved the ladder into one of the open spaces. When he finished he straightened, wiped his hands down his thighs and looked at me.

"You gonna open that?"

I looked down at the plastic bag I still held. "Am I supposed to?"

"It's your stuff," he said. "The stairs aren't safe. I used that," he flicked his head at the place he had slid the ladder, "went through the window and got some of your things. The apartment looks good, just some stuff out of the cupboards in the kitchen. I picked it up and set it on the counter. Anyway, I grabbed some of your stuff, thought you might want it," he tipped his chin at the bag in my arms.

Tears stung my eyes and I blinked several times.

"Thanks," I said.

"No problem," he said, and looked uncomfortable. "You're gonna have to stay in the motor home for a few more days. I brought some groceries. They're in the truck." He turned away, towards the gate. "Take me a few minutes. The truck is around on the side street, so I could get to your window. I'll be back in a little bit."

I walked back to the motor home, eager to have my own things and curious at the same time as to what was in the bag. I stepped inside and flipped the lights on. Setting the bag on the floor by the table I opened it and reached inside.

The first handful I pulled out was underwear – bras and panties. I blushed looking at them, knowing that Patrick Murphy had been in my underwear drawer. At the same time I was so happy to see my underwear that tears again burned my eyes. I set them on the table and looked in the bag. It contained tee shirts, two pairs of jeans, socks and in the bottom my other pair of sneakers.

I sat down on the bench seat, snuggled my sneakers to my chest like a lost child and looked at the pile of clothes. Hearing the engine of his truck pull up I gathered my clothes and carried them to the back, dumping them on the bed. I slid the folding door closed and hurried up to the front. I got to the door just as Patrick knocked. Swinging it open I stood aside to let him in. He had to turn sideways to get through the narrow door because he had a brown grocery bag in each arm. He set them on the table.

"That's just some basic stuff," he said. "Hold you a couple of days till you get to a store." He reached in the first bag and pulled out a loaf of bread, a jar of peanut butter and a jar of strawberry jam. A package of sliced ham, another of cheese slices and a jar of mustard joined the bread. Peering inside he said, "There's milk and cereal. Hope you like corn flakes."

"Let me pay you," I said. "This is too much."

"No need. You're stuck with things I like to eat. Anything you don't like, I'll eat next week. Is that my tee shirt?"

Looking down I realized I was still wearing his shirt. "Yeah," I said. "I borrowed it. I didn't have anything clean."

He looked me up and down. "That's strange."

I looked down, too. No spots or stains. "What's strange?"

"I never noticed those bumps in it before. Not when I wore it."

My cheeks flamed. His laugh filled the small space where we stood.

With a smile that lit those blue eyes he tipped my chin up. "I'm sorry, Marlena, I couldn't resist. You are so cute when you blush."

I've been called a lot of things over the years. Cute was not one of them.

I shrugged away from his hand and turned to the remaining bag of groceries. A bottle of wine, a can of coffee and a liter of Coke. A toothbrush and toothpaste. A new hair brush and comb set. "Well, you're here. How about dinner? I can offer you a ham sandwich or peanut butter and jelly."

"I have a better idea. How about you put on one of your own shirts and I take you to dinner? Thursday night is chicken and dumplings at Kelly's."

"I would love that," I said. "As long as you let me buy your dinner."

"How 'bout we arm wrestle for it?"

I smiled, looking at the biceps filling the sleeves on his tee. "I can do that," I said.

His eyes glinted in the soft light. "I bet you can. Come on, change your shirt. Let's go eat."

I grabbed the rest of the clothes, the toothbrush and the hair brush. "Be right back," I called over my shoulder. I went to the sleeping area and pulled the folding door across the aisle.

Patrick's laugh followed me. I yanked his shirt over my head and picked up one of mine, pulling it on. I sat long enough to run the brush through my hair.

Sliding the door open I went up front.

"I put the stuff away. Nice thing about a motor home, if you can't find something, it's never that far away. Compact," he said when I joined him. "You ready?"

I nodded. He stepped aside and gestured me ahead of him. As I passed him he swatted my fanny.

"That's sexual harassment," I said. "You're my boss."

"No it wasn't. That door was swinging open. I was hurrying you along so you didn't get hit."

I laughed in spite of myself, feeling lighter than I had in days. "You, sir, are full of soft brown stuff."

"No, sir's my dad. I'm Patrick." He opened the door to the truck and helped me in, leaning across my lap to snap the seat belt.

Straightening again, he snapped his fingers. "Dang, no blush."

I laughed again.

We drove over the ridge into Monarch with the radio blaring country songs and singing along. I was surprised. He had a very good singing voice and he knew all the words. At Kelly's he held the door and guided me in with one hand on the back of my waist.

We took a booth in the back and sat across from each other.

Although I hadn't known Patrick very long I knew the difference between this guy and the first one I met. And I liked this guy. We laughed and talked through dinner without ever mentioning the facility or the earthquake. When Kathy came to clear the table Patrick looked at me. "Dessert? Pie is real good here."

"I'm stuffed, thanks. You go ahead."

"Coffee?"

"I'll take coffee."

"Good. Two coffees and what kind of pie is left?"

The pretty waitress smiled. "There might be a piece of pecan pie put back for some lonely bachelor."

"Dang," Patrick said. "Lost out to the lonely guy. How about cherry?"

For a moment Kathy looked stunned, surprised or something. "I'll get that for you."

"And two coffees."

"Yes, sir," she snapped and turned to the front, her feet slapping on the linoleum.

I looked up at Patrick. "Problem?"

"Not for me. How about you?" He smiled, folding his hands in front of him.

"I'm fine," I said. "Thank you for dinner."

"Thank you. I thought you were paying."

I froze for a minute, then reached back for my card case.

Patrick's rich laugh rumbled across the table. "I was kidding, Marlena. Wanted to see if I could get one more blush out of you before I took you home." His eyes were as warm as the sky on a summer day as he smiled at me. "Thank you. For having dinner with me."

Kathy interrupted and slapped a piece of pecan pie in front of him. "Coffee will be right up," she said.

I watched those same eyes chill like a cold wind. "You know what? Cancel that coffee and bring me a box. I'll take it to go. And the check."

"Fine." She snatched up the pie and stormed away from the table, hips snapping side to side, feet still splatting the floor.

Patrick watched her go, then turned to look at me. "I'm sorry about that. For the record, before you jump to the wrong conclusion, that woman has been flirting with me since I got back. It is not a mutual attraction."

"Not my business, Patrick."

He looked into my eyes for a long minute before Kathy slapped a white Styrofoam box in front of him and threw the check on top of it.

With an angelic smile Patrick thanked her. The waitress stood for another few seconds, then went back up front.

"Ready?"

I nodded, slid out of the booth and stood. Patrick handed me the white box, slid his hand to the back of my waist and nudged me forward. I waited at the register while he dealt with the bill, exchanging pleasantries with the other waitress.

Kathy was nowhere in sight.

When we were headed back over the hill to Jade he turned down the radio. "I have a history in this town," he began. "One I didn't earn or ask for. I don't know what you've heard." He glanced at me. "It isn't true. The old timers, they get a hold on something, twist it, shine it up, and put it out there for truth. The ladies grab it up, put a little frosting on it and pass it on around. The only thing I'm guilty of is being good looking. I can't help the way I look."

I listened quietly. Why was he telling me? I admit I had heard a lot of stories about Patrick Murphy and none of them were flattering. All of them referred to him as "Trick". There were various definitions of why the nickname and those, too, were far from flattering.

The man I had just shared dinner with was a far cry from the man in the stories.

"What?" He asked, giving me another glance.

"I didn't say anything."

"I noticed. Why? What are you thinking?"

I sighed. "I was thinking how much I enjoyed our dinner. You were right – that chicken and dumplings is the best I've ever eaten."

He laughed again, returning to the man who had shared my dinner. "You eat a lot of chicken and dumplings at home? Growing up?"

I laughed, too. "I ate a lot of fish and a lot of rice. Depending on who was cooking, a lot of beans. Either way, a lot of spice."

"Sounds good," he said. "I was expecting burritos and enchiladas."

250

"Yep, that too." I explained my mixed parentage and the battle for the kitchen. He laughed in all the right places, was serious when I talked about losing my dad. By the time I finished we were back at the storage facility.

Patrick pulled up to the gate, punched in his code and the gate slid smoothly back on its track. He drove back to the motor home and parked in front of it. I waited while he came around and opened my door, extending his hand to take the white box and help me down.

I pulled his key out of my back pocket and opened the door to the motor home, reaching inside and turning on the dim interior lights. I turned to hand him the box of pie.

"Keep it," he said, sliding his arms around my waist. "I just wanted an excuse to spend more time with you."

What do you say to that? The air seemed charged, electric, as we looked at each other. Even in the dark his eyes gleamed.

There was a shushing sound, like someone dragging something heavy across the asphalt, the gritty sound of gravel popping.

We both looked towards the buildings.

"What was that?"

"I don't know," he said, his voice low. "I didn't see anything when we pulled in. Stay here. Get inside and lock the door."

"I'm going with you," I said, stepping inside long enough to put the box of pie on the table.

"Wait here," he said softly and hooked an arm around to catch the door. "Lock the door, turn off the lights."

I did an eye roll he couldn't see and turned off the lights.

"Stay here, Marlena. It's probably a raccoon shopping in mom's boxes." I noticed he kept his voice barely above a whisper.

"Then I'll go with you, in case he needs help bagging."

He sighed and tugged on the door. "I'll be back as soon as I show him the gate. Lock up. Please."

The last sounded almost painful. I don't think he used that word much.

"All right. I'll make some coffee to go with that pie."

He shook his head. "Keep the lights off till I get back."

"Don't forget to come back. I don't want to sit here in the dark wondering if you're all right."

"I won't forget," he said, and pulled again on the door.

I let go and the door closed with a snick. I went between the captain's chairs in the cabin and looked out the windshield. Patrick went across the drive and blended into the deeper shadows beside Building Seven. In a minute I lost him completely.

I waited for maybe ten minutes. No sign of him, no sounds. No sounds I could hear anyway. I backed out of the cabin and went to the dining area. Did he leave? No. His truck was still outside. I would have heard it start.

No cloud cover tonight. The harbor lights reflect off the cloud cover to provide a dim light. With no moon it was very dark outside, barely lighter than the inside of the motor home. The facility lights were all out, from those on the buildings to the perimeter lights. None of them came on when darkness settled in for the night.

Careful with the door I opened it and stepped outside. I waited, breathing slowly, and listened. Moving on my toes I made my way alongside Pat's truck. When I was between the truck's bed and the nose of the motor home I paused and listened again.

Something wasn't right.

By my watch it had been twenty minutes since Patrick went to check on a noise. I could circumvent the whole facility in that time. I hurried across the drive to the area that swallowed Patrick earlier.

Staying in the darkest strip, alongside the building, I tiptoed forward to the corner letting my eyes adjust to the dark. Pausing at the corner I held my breath and listened again.

A faint noise, almost a white noise, came from Building Three. I crossed the aisle as quickly and as silently as I could and took up the same position beside Building Five. At the next corner I paused again and listened.

Something was in front of Building Three, the next one over. I couldn't make out what it was. I used the trick of looking to the side of it rather than straight at it. It looked like boxes. Stacks of boxes.

I heard footsteps crunching on the pebbles of the asphalt. A grunt. I dropped to my knees, bent over and got as close to the ground as I could. Easing my head forward I looked around the corner.

A dark pickup truck was parked in the aisle, close to the fallen roof. A dark figure stood in the bed of the truck and another lifted something over the tailgate. Another grunt. The one on the ground bent, picked something up and lifted it. I couldn't make out their features, it was too dark.

A whisper sounded loud in the silence. "Hang on a second," it hissed. I made out the words clearly. The figure behind the truck turned towards me and I ducked back, staying close to the ground, making myself as small as I could, breathing through my mouth.

I watched as Paul Murphy materialized out of the darkness. He was less than fifteen feet from me when he stopped. I thought he might be looking around so I hugged the ground, wishing I could see him better, be sure it was Paul. He turned around and went back towards the truck.

I lost him in the darkness. It was like watching a ghost materialize and fade.

There was no sign of Patrick.

I wondered if he was maybe helping Paul load something but why wouldn't he let me know? The figure in the truck bed had looked too short to be Pat but it was hard to tell in the dark. I got to my knees, one hand on the building to keep my balance and eased upright.

Light suddenly blazed at me, blinding me. I put up a hand to block it and still saw stars. "Hello, Marlena."

Paul Murphy. I knew the voice although my eyes were still seeing yellow stars.

"What's going on? I heard noises," I said, and got to my feet.

"Where did you come from? I thought you were staying at the motel."

I shook my head, blinking rapidly, trying to avoid the light.

"No, I was here," I said.

"I see that," he said, and dropped the light from my face. It shone in a yellow puddle at my feet, the outer edges lighting a stack of cartons next to the corner of Building Three. I watched the light draw closer, heard his footsteps close in on me. "What are you looking for?"

"Me?" I stalled. "I wanted to know what that noise was. Did you hear it?"

Enough light reflected off the ground and the cartons that I could see Paul behind the flashlight he held. "You didn't answer me, Marlena. Where did you come from? Why are you spying on me?"

"Spying? I wasn't spying on you, Paul. I heard a noise and came to see what it was."

"Came from where. Last time I'm gonna ask."

I gestured with my hand. "From the motor home."

"What's going on?" Behind him, from the direction of the truck, Burke spoke. "Who are you talking to?"

Paul stepped closer and flashed his light on me. "Look who I found spying on us."

"Marlie? What the hell are you doing here?"

"I could ask you the same thing, Burke." Burke was dressed in black but even the faint reflection of light glinted on his bright blonde hair. "What are you doing here? The gates are closed. No one is coming in tonight."

"Checking on things, making sure the facility is secure," he said, hopping down from the truck bed. "I ran into Paul and gave him a hand. He's trying to get his mom's things moved. Take them up to the house."

I glanced back at Paul. "Why now? Why not wait till daylight? That roof can let go completely. Kinda dangerous to be in there in the dark."

"It's braced pretty well on those boxes," he said. "I got in, shoved some out and Burke stacked them. Mom is real worried about her stuff."

In the dark? I wasn't buying it. And where was Patrick?

I moved towards the truck bed and Burke caught my arm.

"What?" I asked him, tugging my arm free. Paul shone the flashlight on me. The light reflected off me and onto the cartons already loaded. Enough to see the packing tape with the three main strings running through it. Not enough light to see the colors but enough to see the pattern of those reinforcing strings.

"Get that light out of here," Burke snapped, slapping Paul's hand. The beam of light went up, spun wildly across the corner of the building then hit the ground and went out to the sound of shattering glass. Without that narrow beam of light the dark wrapped around us.

Paul started cursing at Burke.

"Grab her," Burke ordered.

Acting on pure instinct I took off, up on my toes, digging in and trying not to make noise. I sprinted for the next building and got around the corner before I heard the slap of feet on the asphalt. I flattened against the wall, mouth open, trying not to make a sound.

"Find her?" Burke's voice, from behind me.

"Not yet. Watch the gate!" Paul yelled from somewhere ahead, near the motor home. "Turn the truck lights on. Give us some light in case she tries to circle back."

I held my pose till my heart quit pounding. Then I was up on my toes and moving again, as fast as I could run.

I ran for the back of the lot, away from both of them. I cut left as soon as I hit the cross aisle and waited again, stuck close to the back of the building.

The next aisle suddenly lit up. No way could I get across there without being seen. Behind me I heard faint footsteps coming my way. I turned and ran the other way, across that aisle and then hooked another left and ran for the back of the lot.

Behind the buildings I could stay in the dark and watch for their silhouettes against the walls, as long as the headlights stayed on. There was a narrow track there, between the back of buildings and the fence.

The best thing about long legs is how far they will carry you in full flight. I cleared the corner of Building Eight and slowed, feeling my way along the fence till I found the last outdoor slot. Ed White kept his boat in this space, a smaller cabin cruiser.

I felt for the tongue on the trailer then felt my way up to where the hull rested. Climbing carefully, trying not to make a noise, I caught the top rail and pulled myself up until I could swing a leg up and catch the side rail.

Using my left hand and my heel I pulled myself up and got a grip on the deck rail. I managed to get my right arm around the rail and pull myself upright.

I heard Paul yell something but couldn't make out the words. If Burke answered him I didn't hear it. I managed to roll between the rails and drop onto the deck. I misjudged the drop and my sneakers hit the wood with a thunk that sounded to me like thunder.

I froze again, breathing through my mouth, trying to stay quiet. My throat was dry from the sprint and the open mouth breathing. I could feel a cough coming. Turning my head into my shoulder I tried to muffle it. Then I waited some more.

After a few minutes I heard an engine. I saw a faint light on the wall across the aisle, watched it gain intensity as the truck came closer. Another light played back and forth, across and back, up and down. A spotlight on the truck. The sound of the truck came closer, the big engine rumbling down the aisle, echoing off the walls of the buildings. I waited.

"Marlie? Come on out, babe. What's the matter with you?" Burke's voice. Calling over the rumble of the truck. Minutes went by. I waited. Burke waited. I wondered where Patrick had gone. Was he, too, playing cat and mouse out here? Or had he gone on home wherever that was.

I took a chance and lifted my head a little to see what was happening.

"Marlie?"

Burke sounded so close I dropped my head again.

"What on earth is wrong with you? Come on, babe. I'm worried about you. Let's go get a pizza and talk."

I stayed where I was.

I heard footsteps crackle along the drive.

"Did you find her?"

It was Paul.

"No," Burke snapped. "I told you to watch the damn gate! She'll run that way."

"Well, expert, why didn't you know she was here? She said she was staying in your motor home. Don't you keep track of your damn women?"

"Not in my motor home," Burke said. "I have all the keys. Come on, let's get loaded and get out of here. She may already be out the gate. I don't want to get caught with this."

"Give me a lift."

I heard the door of the truck open and slam shut. The gears shifted and slowly the sound faded along with the light. I waited until the darkness was solid again before I pushed myself to a sitting position and took a deep breath.

Burke asked a good question – what was going on? I didn't even know why I ran, let alone why they were hunting me.

And where was Patrick? Thinking about it I realized he couldn't have left. His truck was parked by the motor home. Unless he walked off and left it, he was still here.

Being as quiet as possible I climbed over the rail and dropped back to the asphalt. Staying low I made my way along the row of boats and cars by feel, moving slowly, counting the spaces as I went. Blessings of a good memory, I remembered what was in each space. If I was right, I should be coming up to another aisle.

Across that and up this row should bring me to the end of the row where Patrick's motor home was parked. If his truck was still there, I'd know he was still on the property. For that matter, he might be in the motor home right now, wondering where I went.

I came to the end of this row and stopped to listen. I could hear faint sounds coming from the right. I sprinted across the aisle and slipped under the boat trailer in space 9. The next two spaces were cars. I went behind them, easing along the fence. Space 12 was empty and if I was right space 13 held another boat, an aluminum dinghy flat on the ground without a trailer. That one I had to feel for in the darkness. It would sound like a cannon going off if I ran into it.

Burke called out suddenly, sounding very close. "He's gone! I told you to tie him up!"

Paul answered from somewhere further away. I couldn't make out his words.

"Well, it's too late now," Burke snarled. "Get the last of it and let's get out of here. Did you take his phone?"

Another muffled answer.

The sound of Burke's cussing faded away.

Who was gone? Who was tied up? This whole thing was beyond me. Sound travels, especially at night when the air is heavier.

Burke had surprised me, sounding much too close.

I picked up my speed, my hands out in front of me, hoping I would have time to stop when I felt the boat.

Luck was with me. I touched the boat before I ran into it. Dropping to the ground again I felt along its sides where it laid on the ground. It was stored upside down, to keep from holding rain. If I could get under it, I could wait them out. Wait for daylight.

I scooted along on my knees, being as quiet as I could, the bits of gravel biting into my knees as I moved first one then the other. I felt the edge of the boat begin to curve and knew I was close to the bow. The point of the bow held the upturned boat off the ground.

I slid my fingers along the edge until I could feel a space between the boat and the ground. I tried to lift it, get an idea how heavy it was.

An aluminum boat can't be that heavy, can it?

Well, yes it can. Trying to lift it meant getting up on my knees, into a kneeling position. I didn't have enough arm strength to lift the boat. I needed to get to my feet, use my legs.

And then what? There was no way I was going to be able to stand, lift the boat and slide under it at the same time.

I felt further, trying to see if there was enough clearance for me to slide under without lifting it. No go. Hard to judge in the dark but it felt like eight inches or so, not enough for my fanny to clear.

Frustrated, I crossed my ankles and sat down, giving my knees a break. If I could find a block of some kind maybe I could lift the boat, slide the block under the edge to hold it up and then get under it.

Maybe I could just call MacGyver. Or give Superman a buzz.

I dropped my elbows to rest on my spread knees and let my shoulders slump and my head hang loose to relieve some of the tension.

What was happening? My mind spun from did I hear something to where's Patrick to was that a noise and back to what is going on. Why am I hiding? More confusing, why was I running from Burke?

Burke, my pal, my buddy, always the flirt, always affectionate. Did he really want more? Maybe he was sincere. Maybe he was involved with Paul in something else, something beyond high school friends.

I watch TV. I'm neither stupid nor blind. I saw those cartons they had loaded in the truck and I recognized them, at least a couple of them. Burke is helping Paul or vice versa to move cartons marked exactly like the cartons of drugs.

Maybe the bad guys didn't get the missing cartons off the property. Maybe they got moved into one of Mrs. Murphy's units. One like Building Three, with the huge combined space where walls had never been built.

With all of her stuff a few more cartons, or boxes, would never be noticed. She couldn't possibly remember every one of them and what was in it.

I lifted my head, arched my back and stretched those muscles, cooling from sitting cross legged so long.

Arms grabbed me, a hand gripped my face, covering my mouth with a cupped palm. I tried to bite and couldn't reach the palm. I yanked my head forward trying to break loose, my hands trapped by the arm locked around me.

"It's Patrick," a sigh whispered past my ear. "Be still."

I wilted and took in a deep breath. The fingers pressed around my mouth relaxed and let go. My heart hammered so hard in my chest I was afraid the adrenaline surging through my system was audible.

The hand that had been covering my mouth smoothed across my forehead and down my cheek. I felt a warm breath on my cheek, near my ear.

"You okay?" He breathed against my ear.

I nodded, not trusting my voice. He had scared the water out of me.

"I'll lift, you slide under. Stay there. Help on the way."

I thought for a second. If I was under the boat I might be able to lift it using my back, pushing up against one of the bench seats. Could I lift it high enough for him to get under? Was there enough room for both of us beneath the boat? Would pigs fly out my butt?

I shook my head and heard his soft sigh.

Leaning my head back into his chest I felt for his head and pulled it down where I could turn my head and be close to his ear. "No room," I whispered, trying to keep my whisper as soft as his.

His arms left me. Taking my right hand he placed it on the edge of the boat, folding my fingers under it with his.

"Under," he breathed, nudging my back with his chest. I felt him get to his feet, felt his hand move away from mine.

I rolled to my knees, the gravel biting into them again. There was a small sound, a slight hiss in the gravel and the boat began to rise. I felt it with the hand still holding the edge. I got my feet under me and used

263

my legs to lift me inside the circle of Patrick's arms, my back sliding along his body as I stood.

"Under," he whispered.

I shook my head. "You, too."

"Go."

"Well ain't that sweet," Paul said aloud. Bright light lit the scene around us. I flinched from the light and closed my eyes, seeing only a red film. "What'cha doing, guys? Trying to steal a boat?"

Patrick dropped his arms, and the boat, at the same time.

My dad always told me the best defense is a good offense. "What are you doing, Paul? You've been chasing us around all night. What's the game?"

"What's your game, Marlena? You playing a little spy versus spy?"

I leaned back into Patrick. "Trying to get a little action with my man," I said. "You seem bound and determined to mess that up. Want to tell me why?"

Paul snorted and lowered the light a little, getting it out of my face. "Your man?" He laughed. "Honey, you're not even a notch in his belt. Patty likes his little blond fluffs. You know? Those tight bodied little surfer girls with all the bleached blonde hair."

"I'm trying to change that," I said, turning toward him. Paul was only a shape behind the light, hiding in the dark. "He gets a taste of a hot blooded Latina, he'll change his mind. I'm like chili peppers. Cool to the touch, too hot to handle."

Paul chuckled. "I bet you are, Marlena. I know I wanted a taste. You shut me down, remember? Got your little law man sweetie. You know that, Patty? You know she sleeps with that cop Kincaid? She must have a thing for cops. Sleeps with Burke, too. Guess I needed a badge to bed her." He laughed again. "Maybe I can borrow Burke's."

I felt Patrick edging back, away from me, so I shuffled forward a little, turning more towards Paul and further from Patrick. If we could get enough space between us we'd have a chance to jump Paul.

"It's not the badge, Paul. It's the man. Best Burke ever got was a good night kiss. You know, like your first date? Like you say good night to your mother? You kiss your mama, Paulie," I stressed his name, the way his mother always said it. "I've seen you. That's about what it's like to kiss Burke. No fire. Might as well kiss an egg. Lot more responsive."

Paul laughed again. "I knew he was lying. He never was good with the women. They were all mine. One place he never could beat me was with the women. I proved that. A lot."

"I don't know," I said and eased a few more inches left. "You *gringos* not so good in the sheets. I like me a man, you know? *Mucho hombre.*"

Patrick lunged at Paul.

Paul shot him.

There was a flash of yellow, a pop and Patrick fell through the beam of light, slamming into the ground. He never made a sound.

"Pat!" I squatted beside him.

"Get up, Marlena. NOW!"

I stood, my anger rising with me. "You are bad," I said, curling my lips. "I like that, Paulie. You are a man." I eased a little closer to him, smiling more, dropping my eyelids to what I hoped was a sexy look. *"Muy bueno, hombre."* I was using up what little Spanish I had.

I knew Paul spoke Spanish, I had heard him on his cell phone.

I took another step closer and licked my bottom lip. *"Caliente,"* I murmured, hoping that meant hot and not just a hot sauce. I lifted my right hand and slowly, carefully reached toward his face. "You like hot sauce, Paulie?"

His eyes darted from my face to my hand. This close I could see the glint of the gun in his right hand, the light in his left.

I licked my lips again, watched his eyes drop and brought up my knee as hard and fast as I could, right in his jewels. My knee connected with soft tissue and I grabbed for the gun.

Paul mewed like a kitten and dropped, his hands going for his crotch, easily giving me the gun and dropping his flashlight.

I stepped back and aimed the gun at him.

"Nice move, Marlie. Damn, girl, that was hot. Now drop it."

Burke.

His light lit me up.

"Drop it, babe, or I will put a bullet in the back of Trick's head."

I glanced his way, unable to see him clearly with him in the dark and me in the light.

"Come on, Marlie. I've done it before. Give up the gun or he's dead."

I let released the butt of the gun, let it roll forward on my finger.

"Good girl. Put it on the ground. Easy."

I knelt slowly, my hand out, the gun dangling from my forefinger. I kept my eyes on Burke. "You win, Burke. You're the hero. You broke up the drug ring. I'm proud of you," I said, and leaned a little to put the gun where he was shining the light.

"Too late, babe. I'm smarter than Paul. His head is way below his belt. Put the gun down. Now. Or Trick gets it."

I turned my hand a little to the side, almost horizontal, the gun butt touching the ground.

I lunged to the left, gripped the gun and shot Burke.

Twenty years in the Army – I can march and I can shoot. I heard him grunt once then hit the ground. The flashlight he held rolled free, a kaleidoscope of light spun across the asphalt and the boat behind us.

I rolled too, away from him, still holding the gun. The smell of cordite was thick. Paul groaned in the dark. Maybe the gunfire would shut him up.

I pulled my knees up and lifted onto one of them, my right leg out for balance. Getting to my feet, I eased back, away from the light and closer to the building behind me. Burke made no sound at all.

Moving in a wide circle I tried to get behind the flashlight. If I could pick it up I had the advantage. Right now, the dark was my friend. I put out a foot, shifted my weight to it and brought up the other.

Slow but steady.

I was shifting forward again, my weight balanced on both legs, when another light bloomed from the ground and a bullet nicked my left calf.

I dove again, scraping my hands but keeping the gun and rolling. I rolled toward the boat, or where I thought the boat was, trying to keep my eyes aimed at the spot the shot came from.

All I could hear was the sound of my clothes against the asphalt as I rolled, still clutching the gun in my right hand.

I must have rolled ten or twelve feet by the time I stopped, my mouth wide open, trying to breathe without making a noise.

My elbows stung as I rested on them, bringing my left hand up to support the right one with the gun in it. I eased in a deep breath, drawing it in as far as I could before letting it out.

The flashlight on the ground shone against the stucco of the building, creating a dim, pale glow. It reflected onto the asphalt below but it was very little light. I looked away and closed my eyes. I tipped my watch to see what time it was and couldn't see it. I brought my left hand up and touched my cheek with face of the watch.

It was broken. I felt the rough edges on my skin. I put my left hand back on the butt of the gun. Another deep breath.

There was a scuffling sound and Paul groaned again. At least I thought it was Paul.

I waited, letting my legs relax, wiggling my toes, anything to stay loose for a minute or so. Another sound. Maybe a sigh? A deep breath? I tightened my legs again, renewed my grip on the gun.

"Good shot," Burke's voice called from the dark. "Damn near hit me. Now come on out. Don't make me kill Trick. I like the guy, babe. I like you. A lot, Marlie. Let's talk, okay?"

I stayed quiet, trying to locate Burke by his voice. Harder than you think when you're lying flat on the ground in the dark.

"Marlie? I know you hear me. Come on, this is ridiculous. Look. I'll stand up, okay? Show a little faith, babe. I'll stand up, you stand up. No guns. All right? I'll go first. Can you see anything? Marlena, come on! Let's talk."

Steeling myself, I called out. "Okay, Burke," and rolled to the right as fast as I could. Yellow flame sparked before I made the first revolution. I fired three shots at the spot I saw the flame and rolled some more.

Then I waited.

The smell of cordite returned, stinging my eyes.

What seemed like half an hour was probably minutes when I heard another groan. This one sounded tight, like someone had locked their jaw and gritted their teeth, trying not to make a sound.

I rolled another couple of times, my feet bumped against something. The boat? Was I that far already?

I was clear of the slight glow from the flashlight shining against the building. I used my wrists to push my torso upright, finally getting back to my knees. Making as little noise as possible I got to my feet. They tingled, the sudden shift in blood flow rushing to them.

I flexed my toes, my thighs and my butt. I didn't feel anything. I wasn't hit.

Chapter 24

Headlights flashed, red and blue pulsating lights lit up the area. A silver pickup came up one aisle and a black and white squad car came up the other. Vehicle doors opened, men shouted and I heard footsteps coming fast.

A flashlight lit me up again. Then another.

"Drop the gun! Now!"

I lowered my arm, the blood tingling through my hand as I released my hold on the gun and let it flip upside down. I let it dangle from my forefinger again.

John Kincaid stepped out of the glare to take the gun. "You all right, Marlena?"

"Yeah," I said, my voice sounding rusty. "Where did you come from?"

He slipped an arm around my shoulders. "Patrick called," he said. "Made it as fast as I could. Had to call the dispatcher for the gate code. Good thing you gave us one."

"Patrick," I said, raising my hands and rubbing my face. "He may be hurt. Over there somewhere," I pointed and followed my own direction. "I think he's in this aisle."

Another officer called out. "Two men down here," he said. "I called for an ambulance."

John took control. "Watkins, go open the gate for them. Who's down, Chuck?"

"Code 871," I said. "That will open the gate and lock it open."

Officer Watkins waved and jogged toward the gate.

John led me to the squad car and opened the back door. "Sit down, Marlena. You sure you're all right? Do you want medical assistance?"

"I want to know if Patrick is okay. I think Burke shot him."

"Where is Burke?"

"Somewhere around here. I shot him."

"You shot Burke?"

"Yeah. Pretty sure I hit him. At least once."

"You up to looking? Chuck says there's two men down."

I stood up again. He took my arm and turned me toward the fence. In the garish light strobing the aisle I saw another officer on one knee beside a prone body.

He stood up when we reached him and shook his head.

"He's gone."

I sucked in my breath, tears stinging my eyes.

John kept an arm around me, let me take my time.

I looked into Burke's eyes, still open.

The front of his sweatshirt was black and shiny, the flashing red lights reflecting in little glints.

"Where's Patrick?" I asked.

"Over here," John said and used a hand on my waist to guide me to the corner of the building.

The hot tears rolled down my cheeks.

Patrick Murphy sat on the ground, leaning back against the stucco wall. One side of his face was darkened but his eyes were open, the red light flashing in them.

He lifted a hand and held it out, palm up.

I put my hand in it. He tugged on it and I knelt beside him.

A siren wailed in, more flashing red lights. One of the officers was calling orders.

"Hey," I said, leaning close to him. "How you doing?"

Patrick blinked a few times. "I've been better. How about you?"

"I'm good. Better than you, I think. You hurt?"

He smiled. "My head and my pride. My body is fine."

"I'll say," I smiled back and winked.

"Now you want to start something," he said. "First I want to, and you don't. Now you want to and I can't. We've got to get on the same page."

"What makes you think I want to start something?"

He lifted his chin and looked at me. "I'm gonna find out," he said. "Give me a hand up?"

I stood and pulled on his hand, the one I was holding, and watched him get to his feet. He tilted to the right, away from me and I caught his arm to help him get his balance.

An EMT came up to us.

"Check her first," Patrick said.

I let go of his hand and held up mine. "I'm okay," I said. "He's hurt. His head."

"Can you sit down for a minute?" the EMT asked. "Let me get a look at your head."

"I just got up," Patrick said.

"This way then," the EMT said, as he took Patrick's elbow. He led him towards the flashing lights of the ambulance, the inside cabin lit up bright white.

Patrick flailed one hand back towards me. "Come on."

"I'll be right there. I have to talk to John first."

Together they walked to the ambulance. I watched them for a few seconds. Patrick was steady on his feet.

I turned around and looked for John.

I found him beside Burke's body.

I walked over to stand beside John.

John shook his head. "He's gone, Marlie."

I looked down into Burke's face. The lights flashed highlights into his bright blonde hair. Still handsome, the blue eyes stared into the night sky unblinking, those sculpted lips slightly open.

He looked like he might jump up and ask for a beer. I knelt beside him and closed his eyes.

"*Vaya con Dios*," I whispered.

I stood up and walked away, back towards the bright lights of the ambulance.

The back door of the squad car was still open. Paul Murphy sat there, hunched over with both hands in his lap. The light reflected off the handcuffs.

I passed him and went to the ambulance, where Patrick sat on the gurney inside. An EMT bent over his head.

He caught me looking in and leaned away from the guy swabbing his head.

"Give me a minute," I heard him say. "I'll be right back." He stood up and came to the back of the ambulance. Using the handles on the door he gingerly lowered himself to the ground.

"You better get back in there," I said. "You look pretty rough."

Patrick shoved his hands in his pockets and looked at me.

"You look pretty good," he said. "Considering."

"Are you okay?"

"Headache. Sore ribs. Probably be a lot worse tomorrow. How about you? Did he hurt you?"

"Never laid a glove on me," I grinned at him. "I'm fine, Patrick. Few scrapes and scratches. That's it."

He looked into my eyes, held my gaze. "I owe you, Marlena. You saved my life."

"I think we helped each other. Let's call it even."

"I can do that," he nodded. "On one condition."

"You paying for dinner?"

"No. We still have some unfinished business."

"Like what? You gonna fire me?"

He took his hands out of his pockets, lifted them to my shoulders and tugged me closer.

I went with the pull, stepping in close to him, almost touching, our eyes still connecting us.

He slowly dropped his head, his eyes closed and he kissed me. Softly, gently. I slid my arms around his waist and returned the kiss.

He turned it up, his mouth working across mine and I leaned into him, giving it back, holding him tighter.

He finally lifted his head a little, a smile curving his lips. "I've wanted to do that since the first time I saw you blush."

He brought up one hand, brushed it down my cheek, still holding me with his eyes.

"Does that mean I'm not fired?"

He chuckled. "I'm gonna set you on fire," he grinned. "First chance I get."

I grinned at him. "You think you're gonna get that chance?"

"I do."

"I hate to interrupt," John said, coming up behind Patrick. "These guys need to get to work." He aimed a thumb at the EMTs who stood with their arms folded smiling at us. "You going with them, Patrick?"

I stepped back and dropped my arms. "Yes, he is. He needs to be checked. He took a blow to the skull. He may be out of his head."

Patrick laughed. "I don't think so, Marlie. I think my head is finally on straight." He winked, backed up and climbed into the ambulance. He sat on the gurney as the EMT turned back and shut the doors.

I stood with John and watched the ambulance back up, turn and leave. The red lights were turned off, no siren. A good sign. I watched it until it made the turn for the front gate.

The police car, with Paul in the back seat, followed it. No red lights there, either.

"Day late and a dollar short," John said, beside me.

"Me?"

He shook his head and smiled. "No ma'am. Me. Come on, I'll take you to the station and get your statement." He took my elbow and turned me towards his truck. "Then I'll give you a ride to the Emergency Center."

Chapter 25

Over the next week John used our statements and evidence from the scene as well as forensics to put together what happened that night.

Paul and Burke were moving drugs through the storage facility. Paul had keys to everything and a 24 hour code for the gates. A truck brought them from the Mexican border this far and unloaded them into Paul's unit. Other times a panga boat dropped the shipment and they moved it here. Another truck, one of Move It trucks Paul rented, then picked them up and took them from here to San Francisco or Fresno, in the central valley.

Somewhere along the line Burke changed sides. His undercover work was for the other team, alerting them to raids, advising them when the coast was clear. He was the leading suspect in the murder of the two men shot in the back of the head and dumped near the freeway off ramp.

There was a task force, that part was true. A sharing of information by a combined group of law enforcement agencies – DEA, CBI, Sheriff, CHP and local.

It seemed Paul Murphy had caught someone's attention a while back, something he bragged about while drunk. They suspected Burke had covered for him. Somewhere along the line they hooked up. The actual task force – which did not include Burke – was watching both of them. Internal Affairs got on the bus and sent their own man in undercover.

It was them that chased Burke into my Mustang. A raid on a panga boat unloading a shipment was supposed to net him but he got away barely, leaving his shirt behind. Those men chasing him were both DEA agents.

It took a while to gather it all, for it to come together. The real undercover cop Internal Affairs put in place was a gorgeous local bad boy named Patrick Murphy.

Yep, turned out the bad boy was a good guy. Doesn't it just figure?

Paul Murphy was happy to talk once he got a bag of ice and found out Papa wasn't going to pay for his attorney. He named Burke as the hit man who killed the two Mexican drivers. They had left the drugs in the unit when they ran out of space. Burke told him Steve Harris had been killed by accident. Carlos Esquibel, one of the drivers Burke killed, had family and they wanted revenge. Steve paid that price. Had it been a week day, it would have been me.

Paul traded everything he knew for a lighter sentence and still went away for ten years.

Mrs. Murphy took to her bed and stayed there. Until all the buildings were repaired. Then the thought of all that empty space wooed her back. Patrick supervised the rebuilding and made sure three new walls divided that large space into four units. Two of those were rented to paying customers before Mrs. Murphy could lay claim.

Papa Murphy sold the facility to a chain who brought in one of their own managers to manage the place.

I got thirty days' notice and a nice severance package from the new owners.

The forensics report took weeks. John Kincaid tried to protect me from the findings but someone leaked them and I found out.

The shots I took at Burke had all been hits. There were four bullets in him, all from the gun I laid on the ground for John. That first one hit him. The other three finished him.

An inquest was held once all the reports and evidence was collected. Paul was brought in from prison to testify, a part of his agreement. I testified, too. John Kincaid gave his statement.

I was exonerated and no charges were filed.

The insurance company refused to pay for the Mustang, claiming the earthquake was an Act of God.

I was okay with that, not wanting the memory of Burke throwing himself into the front seat and threatening my life with a comb.

There were times I missed him. Missed his easy laugh, those dancing eyes and the sunshine on his bright blonde hair as he swept the lot.

I thought of him every time an old movie came up on cable. I rarely watched them now. I switched to cop shows and action flicks.

And westerns.

Patrick loves westerns.

59462050R00162

Made in the USA
San Bernardino, CA
05 December 2017